Beauty or Brains?

The only light in Lavina's room came from a small silver-gilt candelabrum.

Before she blew out the candles she had one more look at the lovely room.

To her astonishment, the mirror on the other side of the mantelpiece swung open and the Marquis came into the room.

"It was not possible to say good-night properly with so many people around us," he said.

Lavina felt a strange breathless sensation.

"Please . . ." she said, "go away . . . you know you . . . should not . . . be here. . . ."

A Camfield Novel of Love by Barbara Cartland

———

"Barbara Cartland's novels are all distinguished by their intelligence, good sense, and good nature. . . ."

— ROMANTIC TIMES

"Who could give better advice on how to keep your romance going strong than the world's most famous romance novelist, Barbara Cartland?"

— THE STAR

Dearest Reader,

Camfield Novels of Love mark a very exciting era of my books with Jove. They have already published nearly two hundred of my titles since they became my first publisher in America, and now all my original paperback romances in the future will be published exclusively by them.

As you already know, Camfield Place in Hertfordshire is my home, which originally existed in 1275, but was rebuilt in 1867 by the grandfather of Beatrix Potter.

It was here in this lovely house, with the best view in the county, that she wrote *The Tale of Peter Rabbit*. Mr. McGregor's garden is exactly as she described it. The door in the wall that the fat little rabbit could not squeeze underneath and the goldfish pool where the white cat sat twitching its tail are still there.

I had Camfield Place blessed when I came here in 1950 and was so happy with my husband until he died, and now with my children and grandchildren, that I know the atmosphere is filled with love and we have all been very lucky.

It is easy here to write of love and I know you will enjoy the Camfield Novels of Love. Their plots are definitely exciting and the covers very romantic. They come to you, like all my books, with love.

Bless you,

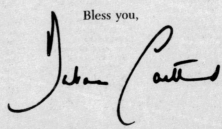

CAMFIELD NOVELS OF LOVE

by Barbara Cartland

Other Books by Barbara Cartland

A NEW CAMFIELD NOVEL OF LOVE BY

BARBARA CARTLAND

Beauty or Brains?

J

JOVE BOOKS, NEW YORK

BEAUTY OR BRAINS?

A Jove Book / published by arrangement with
the author

PRINTING HISTORY
Jove edition / April 1991

ISBN: 0-515-10550-3

Jove Books are published by The Berkley Publishing Group,
200 Madison Avenue, New York, New York 10016.
The name ''JOVE'' and the ''J'' logo
are trademarks belonging to Jove Publications, Inc.

Author's Note

MUSICAL Comedy, which succeeded the old *Burlesque*, opened at the Gaiety Theatre in 1894.

George Edwardes, who was an acknowledged genius of the Theatre, had taken great care over the production of *The Shop Girl*, which was different from anything that had been seen previously.

First Nighters flocking to the Gaiety saw a glittering and exciting show.

They were astounded by the exquisite taste in décor and costumes and they were entranced by the Gaiety Girls who were the perfection of femininity.

The word "Girl" was in the title and the idea of Girl dominated the show.

George Edwardes glorified femininity and he made his Girls acceptable to both men and women alike. He believed above all things in the attraction of the word "Girl."

He put the word in his titles whenever he could and it proved to be a winning decision.

From 1894 to 1914 was the Gaiety Girl period.

They married into the Peerage and were as successful there as they had been on the stage.

I knew well Rosie Boote, who became the charming Marchioness of Headfort, and Denise Orme, who married two Dukes and who was exceedingly beautiful and alluringly feminine right up to her death.

The Shop Girl ran at the Gaiety for 546 performances, setting up a new record at the time.

It was followed by *My Girl* with Ellaline Terriss, who was now the Gaiety's leading lady, but it was not the success of *The Runaway Girl* which followed it and ran for 593 performances.

There would never again be the same excitement over showgirls as there was over the Gaiety Girls.

To the young men of London Society they were the dream of their hearts, and it was each one's ambition to take them out to supper.

There has been nothing like it before or since.

The Gaiety Stage-Door was the Gateway to Romance, but when women became what they called "emancipated," they lost the glamour, the glitter, and the adoration which the Gaiety Girls personified.

Beauty or Brains?

chapter one

1894

THE Marquis of Sherwood stepped out of his exceedingly smart carriage at the door of the Gaiety Theatre.

The Commissionaire saluted him smartly as he walked up the steps and into the vestibule.

There was no question of him showing a ticket; the attendants bowed and smiled as he went up to his own Box.

The Show was in full swing and, as the Marquis took his seat, he saw they were nearing the end of the last act.

He had seen *The Shop Girl* a dozen times already, but he still enjoyed the *Finalé,* in which the Gaiety Girls played a prominent part.

The Marquis, perhaps better than anyone else, understood how George Edwardes, the most brilliant Showman of his time, had swept away *Burlesque* which had been popular for so many years.

Instead, he had introduced Musical Comedy to London.

It had emerged from the Ballad Opera, the Balletta, the Comic Opera, the Musical Farce, and now was a polished, rich, and compelling Show which had made Theatrical history.

George Edwardes had produced a revolution which entranced and mesmerised the whole of London.

Besides his exquisite taste in décor and costumes, the Gaiety Girls were the perfection of feminine elegance.

George Edwardes glorified femininity.

He made his Girls acceptable to men and women alike.

The Gaiety Girls were already famous, and in Musical Comedy gone were the scanty bodices and tights of *Burlesque*.

The Girls were elegantly gowned from their bare skin to the tops of their heads.

It was known to everybody in London that their under-clothes were of pure silk enriched with real lace.

The Marquis glanced around the Theatre and saw that every seat was taken.

As he had invested quite a lot of money in the Show, it was satisfactory to think that not only was George Edwardes' hunch right, but his also.

It was, in fact, the Marquis who had been partly instrumental in making the Gaiety Girls famous.

Because he was one of the most important young aristocrats in Society, there were a great number of men ready to follow his lead when he extolled the Gaiety Girls.

He watched their performance nearly every night, then took one or another of them out to supper.

That became the ambition of every young man who could afford it.

To take a Gaiety Girl to Romano's they would spend every copper they had and walk home bemused and elated with sheer joy.

There had been nothing like it before in the story of the Theatre.

The Gaiety Stage-Door was the Gateway of Romance.

It was always besieged by dozens of young men in top-hats and tails, each praying that he would be fortunate enough to persuade one of the Goddesses he worshipped to have supper with him.

The Shop Girl was, as the Marquis knew, an animated Show which enraptured the audience from the moment the curtain rose.

The first act was set in "The Royal Stores" which lived up to their name.

The second was in "The Fancy-Dress Bazaar" in Kensington.

It was a love-story, a romance in which a young Medical student of "blue blood" falls in love with a mere shop-girl.

As the act before him began to approach the climax, the Marquis thought a little cynically that the story had already been carried out by the Gaiety Girls.

Some of them had married either their titled lover or else a millionaire.

He was quite certain many more would be fortunate enough to end up in the same way.

Quite a number of these alluring, beautiful and exquisitely dressed young women had passed through his hands.

But there was no question of him losing his heart and offering them marriage.

He had long ago decided he would marry nobody until he was too decrepit to enjoy the delights of London.

In the meantime, he was determined not to permit himself to be bored.

It seemed impossible that he should be so, considering how much he possessed.

Those who envied him thought that the whole world was his oyster.

He not only had one of the most famous titles in *Debrett's Peerage,* but he owned one of the finest houses in the country, and a huge estate to go with it.

His race-horses invariably were first past the winning-post and his pack of hounds was undoubtedly the most exclusive.

The curtain came down to rapturous applause and the "Stars" took their calls.

Bouquet after bouquet was brought onto the stage amid the shouts and whistles for the Leading Ladies.

Even more noise greeted the Gaiety Girls.

The Marquis raised his opera-glasses to look more closely at the one he intended to take out to supper.

She was smiling and looked, he thought, exceedingly lovely.

At the same time, some cynical part of his brain

told him that her reign had come to an end as far as he was concerned.

He had to admit, however, that the time they had spent together had been enjoyable.

The curtain fell and the Marquis, knowing it would rise again at least a dozen times, walked leisurely from his Box and down to the Stage-Door.

It was opened for him by an attendant, who greeted him, saying:

"'Evenin', M'Lord! Nice t'see you. It's bin a good Show to-night!"

"So I observed!" the Marquis replied.

He walked through the door and along the somewhat dirty passage to the iron staircase which led to the dressing-rooms.

On his left was the door leading into the street.

Sitting inside his glassed-in office was the eagle-eyed Jung who was, as usual, being besieged by young men begging him to take messages to the Gaiety Girls.

The Marquis thought as he watched them that Jung's pockets were bulging with gold coins which were thrust upon him with the notes they wished him to deliver.

Then, as he waited, he could hear the Orchestra playing *God Save the Queen* and knew the curtain had finally fallen.

Now those on stage came rushing past him.

The women hesitated, smiled, and gave him not only an inviting look, but one which besought him to notice them.

If it was the ambition of every young man to take out a Gaiety Girl, it was the ambition of every Gaiety

Girl to be partnered by the Marquis.

Because she knew better than to keep him waiting, Lucy, the girl he was taking out to supper, soon appeared.

She was certainly very lovely with red hair which owed very little to the artistic talents of her Hairdresser.

Her face could be found in a prominent place in every Stationer's shop-window.

Her figure seemed too perfect to be real.

Her gown was fantastic and accentuated her charms.

As the Marquis knew, it undoubtedly belonged to the Theatre.

He had dressed so many of his mistresses that he was well aware that George Edwardes did not trust their taste.

He invariably allowed them to wear the gowns that he provided when they went to supper at Romano's.

"I hope I've not kept you waiting, M'Lord?"

It was a lisping, soft, feminine voice that asked the question.

Two large eyes looked up pleadingly as she begged him not to be annoyed.

"My carriage is outside," the Marquis said.

He put his hand under Lucy's arm.

As they walked out through the Stage-Door, the crowd outside moved to allow them to pass.

The carriage was the first of a long line drawn up outside.

There were shouts and cheers not only for Lucy, whom they all knew, but also for the Marquis.

"Sherwood!" "Sherwood!" they called out while some of the men shouted:

"Give us a winner!"

It was a cry that the Marquis heard on every race-course.

He acknowledged his public with a wave of his hand before he helped Lucy into the carriage.

She sank down onto the comfortable seat.

Careful as she did so not to dislodge the flowers in her hair which toned with her gown.

As the carriage drove off she said:

"You were late to-night. I missed you."

"I was delayed at my Regimental dinner," the Marquis explained, "and I ought not to have left it, but of course I wanted to see you."

"I've been counting the hours all day," Lucy said, "and they moved very slowly."

The Marquis smiled, but he did not reply.

He had heard innumerable women say the same thing.

In fact, he would have been surprised if they had said anything else.

Driving down the Strand, they drew up outside Romano's Restaurant.

Romano himself, a dark, suave little man, hurried forward to greet the Marquis respectfully.

He led them to a sofa under the balcony.

This, as Lucy knew, was the most important table in the room.

She preened herself, knowing that every woman present in the room was envying her.

They were waving and blowing kisses to the Mar-

7

quis, but as he sat down he did not seem particularly elated.

The oblong room with its dark red curtains and plush sofas was filled with his friends accompanied by extremely elegant women.

Because the applause at the Gaiety Theatre always went on for longer than the other Theatres, almost every other table was full.

Those that were not were awaiting the Gaiety Girls were following the Marquis and Lucy into the Restaurant.

Nearly all of the Girls wore flowers in their hair.

Their *décolletage* was extremely low, their waists so tiny that a man's two hands could easily meet round them.

The Gaiety Girls had special tables kept for them which their admirers decked with flowers.

To-night three of the Girls had huge bells of blossoms over their heads with their names embellished on them.

A waiter brought the Marquis a hand-written menu and the wine-waiter hovered behind him.

He did not hurry in ordering what he wished to eat.

The wine-waiter knew his favourite champagne and had it ready.

As he filled two glasses the Marquis settled himself a little more comfortably on the sofa and said to Lucy:

"Now, what have you been doing with yourself while I have been away?"

"Just waiting for your return," she answered.

"You can hardly expect me to believe that you have

not been out to supper every evening!"

"If I have," she replied, "it has not been with any-one of importance."

She moved a little nearer to him.

But the Marquis was aware that a young man who had just entered the Restaurant was waiting to speak to him.

"Hello, Rupert!" the Marquis said. "I thought you were in the country!"

"I was," the Honourable Rupert Wick replied, "but I thought I might find you here."

"I wanted to see you," the Marquis said. "I thought you would like to shoot with me on the twenty-third."

Rupert Wick's eyes lit up.

He knew it was a privilege to be invited to the Marquis's house, and an even greater one to be in-cluded in one of his shooting-parties.

"I should be delighted to accept," he said, "and incidentally, I have an invitation for you."

The Marquis looked at him questioningly.

"My sister Katherine who, as you may be aware, came out this year, is very eager that you should dine with us one evening."

The Marquis did not answer for a moment, and Rupert Wick went on hastily:

"It will not be a very large party, but Katherine and some of her friends are very eager to meet you."

"I am sure they are," the Marquis said slowly. "But the answer, my dear Rupert, is 'No.' If there is one thing I avoid, it is half-witted, gauche, stupid, and not-well-educated *débutantes*."

He spoke positively, then he smiled.

"Make my apologies to your sister, and I shall look

forward to seeing you on the twenty-third."

Rupert was dismissed, and he knew it.

He knew only too well that it would be useless and embarrassing to argue with the Marquis.

Instead, he walked away to where, across the room, he joined a party of his friends who were entertaining four of the Gaiety Girls.

* * *

Lavina Vernon looked out of the window and saw that it was raining.

She thought that meant she would be unable to ride this afternoon as she had planned to do and was disappointed.

At the same time, she remembered she was halfway through a delightful book.

It described the adventures of a man who had dared to enter Tibet in disguise and who had actually caught sight of the Dalai Lama.

It was not surprising that Lavina enjoyed reading, because the Vicarage was full of books.

Her father, who was the younger son of Lord Vernon, had managed to explore a great deal of the world before he had settled down with a wife.

His father had intended to give him a Parish that was a part of his Estate; unfortunately Lord Vernon died while his son was abroad and the new heir sold the house and its surroundings.

Arthur Vernon was offered a living by the Earl of Kenwick, who had always been a friend of the family.

With his wife, Arthur Vernon settled down at Little Wickington, and they were very happy.

When he could no longer journey abroad as he had

done when he was free, Arthur Vernon "travelled" by reading every book he could find which described parts of the world to which he had not been.

In his spare time he was writing a book himself and to Lavina every chapter seemed more exciting than the last.

She and her father had luncheon together and when they had finished he retired to his Study.

"How did you get on this morning, Papa?" she had asked as they ate the plain but well-cooked food that Lavina's old Nanny had prepared for them.

"I have been doing a little more research on India," her father said. "I think I have got it right now. I will read it to you to-night."

"I shall look forward to that, Papa," Lavina said.

She helped to clear the table and was just about to go upstairs and put on her riding-habit when she realised it was raining.

It was then as she crossed the room to pick up her book that she heard a knock on the front door.

She expected that by this time, Nanny, who was getting on in years, would have retired to her own room to lie down.

Lavina therefore hurried across the hall.

Opening the door, she was surprised to see a smartly attired servant standing there.

He swept off his cockaded top-hat as he asked:

"Is Miss Lavina Vernon at home?"

"Yes, I am," Lavina replied.

The servant ran down the steps and opened the door of the carriage drawn by two horses.

Lavina looked at it in surprise, wondering to whom it belonged.

As the footman held open the carriage door a young woman stepped out.

It was then that Lavina recognised Lady Katherine Wick whom she had not seen for nearly a year.

Lady Katherine, who was looking very attractive and well-dressed, came up the steps.

"Are you surprised to see me, Lavina?" she asked.

"I am delighted!" Lavina answered. "I thought you had forgotten all about me!"

Lady Katherine walked into the hall.

"You must forgive me, dearest," she said, "but I have been in London all the Season, and did not like to intrude when you were in mourning for your mother."

They walked into the Sitting-Room, and Lady Katherine said:

"You are looking lovely, Lavina! If you came to London, you would be a sensation!"

Lavina laughed.

"That is very unlikely. Apart from the fact that Papa has his work to do here, you know as well as I do that we could not afford it."

As Lady Katherine sat down on the sofa Lavina sat down beside her.

"Tell me all about your success during the Season," she begged. "Of course the village has talked of nothing else!"

Lord Wick owned all the cottages in the village and all the land around "Wick House," which was surrounded by a high red brick wall.

Lavina had often thought during the Summer that it was sad to think there was nobody at the Big House.

She had only scraps of information from the various servants who had gone with the Earl to London.

But they all said that Lady Katherine was one of the Beauties of the Season.

It was not surprising, Lavina thought.

She had always admired Katherine not only for her beauty but also because she was a very exciting and adventurous young woman.

She rode brilliantly and would take jumps that even the men thought too risky.

When she was at home she was always organising something amusing for her family and her friends.

She and Lavina had been more or less brought up together.

Lavina had missed the Archery Contests, the canoe races on the lakes, and the cotillions which had been part of every party since she had been a small child.

Now she said:

"I have missed you, Katherine, I have missed you so much!"

"You are making me feel ashamed that I have not communicated with you more often," Katherine replied.

She sounded a little embarrassed as she went on:

"But honestly, Lavina, I was always rushing from one party to another, or else having fittings for gowns until I felt as if my whole body was a pin-cushion!"

Lavina laughed.

"I heard that you were the smartest as well as the most beautiful *débutante* that has ever been seen!"

"That may be an exaggeration," Lady Katherine

said, "but I like to hear it. Now, Lavina, I want you to help me."

"Help you?" Lavina asked.

She looked at Katherine. Then she exclaimed:

"You are up to mischief! I know when you are, and I am never mistaken."

"It may be mischief," Katherine answered, "but it is going to be very enjoyable."

"What is?"

"What I am going to do, and for which I need your help."

Lavina clasped her hands together.

"Tell me all about it."

As she spoke she was surprised to see that Katherine was scrutinising her as if she were inspecting her face and noting every detail.

Then she said:

"You really are lovely, Lavina! I am horrified that I did not ask you to come to London and stay with me so that you could have attended at least some Balls at the end of the Summer when you were out of mourning."

"There was no reason why you should think of me," Lavina replied, "and actually, because I have missed Mama so terribly, I have not really wanted to dance or meet a lot of people, although I am sure she would think it foolish of me."

"Very foolish!" Katherine agreed. "But now you are going to do something amusing, which will make us laugh as we used to do."

"What are you concocting, Katherine? I am sure it is something outrageous."

"It is," Katherine confirmed, "but as we are going

14

to teach a tiresome, conceited, stuck-up man a lesson, we are fully justified in everything we do."

Because of the way Katherine spoke, Lavina gave a little laugh, but she did not interrupt.

"I suppose you have heard of the Marquis of Sherwood?" Katherine asked.

Lavina wrinkled her brow before she replied:

"Yes, of course. He owns a great number of race-horses and has his own pack of fox-hounds."

"That is right." Katherine said. "As he has insulted me, I intend to get even with him."

"Insulted you?" Lavina asked. "How could he have done that?"

"I will tell you," Katherine said. "During the season I made friends with a number of girls who are, to put it frankly, as pretty as I am."

"You are lovely!" Lavina asserted.

"Well, they are lovely too," Katherine said. "We were all fêted, complimented, and made a tremendous fuss of by every important young man in London, with the exception of one."

"That being the Marquis of Sherwood, I suppose!" Lavina smiled.

"You were always very quick-witted," Katherine said, "although he would not believe it!"

Lavina looked puzzled.

"What happened," Katherine went on, "is that I and my friends decided to give a party to which we would invite the Marquis. Everybody knows he is besotted by the Gaiety Girls and appears to take no interest in any other women."

As if she guessed the end of the story, Lavina's eyes twinkled as Katherine went on:

"I persuaded Rupert, who knows him well, to ask the Marquis to our party. I thought if Rupert did so, he would find it difficult to refuse without being rude."

"But he did not accept," Lavina murmured.

"He not only did not accept my invitation," Katherine said, "but he told Rupert he had no use for 'half-witted, gauche, stupid, and not-very-well-educated *débutantes*'!"

"That was certainly very rude!" Lavina remarked indignantly.

"I consider it appallingly bad manners on his part," Katherine said, "and so did my friends. That is why we are determined to get even with him."

"How can you do that?" Lavina asked.

"We have a plan, and that is where you have to help me."

Lavina could not imagine anything she could do as far as the Marquis of Sherwood was concerned.

She thought the story intriguing and therefore listened intently as her friend said:

"We thought about it for a long time, then suddenly I had an idea."

"I was sure it would be you!" Lavina said.

"You know I have always been quick at thinking up something which other people find surprising." Katherine smiled.

"That is true," Lavina agreed. "Do you remember the commotion it caused when you had a performing tiger from a Circus at a party, and it bit your father's favourite dog?"

Katherine laughed.

16

"That, I admit, was a failure. But my other parties have been a success."

"Of course they have!" Lavina agreed. "And they have always seemed to me like something out of a Fairy-Tale."

"That is what I thought," Katherine said, "and what we are going to produce for the Marquis is a Fairy-Tale from which he will wake up to find he has been made to look like an unfortunate clown!"

Lavina could not help feeling that this was unlikely.

But she knew how determined Katherine could be once she had made up her mind about anything.

"I remembered," Katherine said as if she were starting from the beginning, "that the Marquis was infatuated with the Gaiety Girls, and according to Rupert, has never been known so much as to talk to young women like us."

"I can hardly believe that," Lavina said. "If he goes to parties, he is bound to meet them."

"The parties to which he goes are the ones given by the Prince of Wales at Marlborough House," Katherine said, "and by all the older hostesses— witty and sophisticated women who entertain the Professional Beauties."

Lavina knew the Professional Beauties were mobbed by the crowds in the Park and acclaimed everywhere they went.

Until a year ago she had spent a lot of time at Katherine's house and heard her two brothers talking about the delights of London.

She was aware, therefore, that Katherine's elder

brother, the Viscount, was involved with the beautiful Lady deGrey.

Her younger brother, Rupert, spent his time taking the Gaiety Girls out to supper.

"My idea," Katherine was saying, "is that Rupert should persuade the Marquis to give a party at which he would introduce him to Gaiety Girls he has never seen before."

"How can Rupert do that," Lavina asked, "if the Marquis goes to the Gaiety every night?"

"George Edwardes always has a Show on tour," Katherine said. "They visit all the big Towns like Birmingham and Manchester, to find out the faults in the productions and put them right before the Show comes to London. That is why in London they are always a success overnight."

"That is something I did not know," Lavina remarked.

"Rupert told me about it a long time ago," Katherine said, "and when I asked him if it was still happening, he told me that George Edwardes had a Show called *The Girl* travelling about the country now which would take the place of *The Shop Girl* when its run comes to an end."

Lavina wondered how, if Rupert was going to produce the girls who were on tour, it would humiliate the Marquis, which was what Katherine was determined to do.

As if she knew what she was thinking, Katherine said:

"Surely, Lavina, you can guess what I intend to do?"

"I . . . I am . . . sorry," Lavina replied, "but I really have . . . no idea."

"Neither will the Marquis," Katherine said, "but what we are going to do is arrange to stay with him and be introduced by Rupert as Gaiety Girls."

She spoke with an elated note in her voice, but Lavina just stared at her.

"Did . . . you say . . . 'we'?" she asked.

"Of course I said 'we,'" Katherine replied. "It will have to be on the twenty-third because the Marquis will have eight guns shooting that day, and as I already have seven 'Gaiety Girls' including myself, you will be the eighth!"

"You must be crazy!" Lavina cried. "How can I possibly pretend to be a Gaiety Girl? Also, lovely as you are, you could never look like one!"

"Now, do be sensible," Katherine said. "We are not going to appear as we look now. I have been to the Gaiety Theatre several times and I know exactly how they are dressed—in the most exquisite and fantastic gowns. And of course their faces are painted and powdered, their eye-lashes mascaraed and their lips crimson."

Lavina stared at her friend.

"You are not going to look like that!" she retorted.

"I *am* going to look like that, and a great deal more!" Katherine replied. "What we have to do, Lavina, is to convince the Marquis that we are not only lovely to look at, but far more intelligent, far better-educated, and much cleverer than any Gaiety Girl who has ever existed."

Lavina gave a little gasp.

"Is . . . is that possible?"

"We are going to make it possible," Katherine replied, "and if you cannot convince the Marquis and his friends that you are more interesting than some common girl whose only asset is her pretty face, then I will be very disappointed in you!"

"I cannot believe we can really do anything so... outrageous and be... convincing!" Lavina said.

"Then all I have to say is that you have deceived me all these years into thinking you were cleverer than me!" Katherine replied.

Lavina laughed because it sounded so funny. Then she said:

"You are not really... serious about... this, Katherine?"

"Of course I am!" Katherine replied. "I will not have that tiresome, stuck-up man running me down when he has never even met me!"

She made a gesture with her hand before she said:

"Millicent, whose mother is the Duchess of Cumbria, tells me they have invited him to three different parties, and he has never even bothered to reply!"

"That is certainly very rude!" Lavina agreed.

"The Duchess is furious, and so is the Duke!"

"He must go to some parties!" Lavina persisted, feeling somehow the story did not ring true.

"He goes where he thinks he will be amused, which, as I have said, is with much older people than himself, or otherwise he is with the Gaiety Girls, giving them supper at Romano's, where, of course, they shine because there is not much competition."

Katherine's voice was scathing and Lavina knew that what the Marquis had said had made her really angry.

"I am sure," she said tentatively, "you can find somebody better...than...me to...play the... part. I might...make a mess...of it."

"Now you are being silly again," Katherine said. "You know as well as I do that you are cleverer than any of my other friends, and I can remember how well you acted in the Charades we did every Christmas. Rupert said once that you ought to have been an actress."

"Mama would have been horrified at the idea!" Lavina exclaimed.

"Of course you could not really go on the stage," Katherine conceded, "but you could act the part just as if it were a Charade. Then, when we leave, Rupert will tell the Marquis who we really are, and he will realise how stupid he was to be taken in."

"I think...perhaps it is...a mistake..." Lavina began.

Katherine put out her hand to take Lavina's.

"You cannot let me down, Lavina," she said. "You know I have always relied on you, and I will be very hurt and upset if you refuse me."

Lavina drew in her breath.

She felt as if she were taking a very high jump and had no idea what was on the other side of it.

Then as Katherine looked at her pleadingly she said weakly:

"All right...if you want me to...of course I will...help you!"

chapter two

LAVINA and Katherine got into the carriage which was to take them to Wick House.

"I see you have a new footman," Lavina said. "I did not recognise him when you arrived, so I had no idea who was calling on me."

"Papa engaged a lot of new servants in London," Katherine said. "Which means those who have been employed for years will have to 'pull up their socks'!"

Lavina laughed because this was the sort of remark Katherine would make.

At the same time, she knew that the Earl and the whole family were very generous to the village.

Katherine had told her that some of the girls who were to play a part in what she described as a "Dramatic Charade" were staying with her at the moment.

She insisted that Lavina should go back with her

to Wick House to meet them.

"I must tell you what is ... worrying me," Lavina said as they went up the drive with its lime trees on either side.

"What is that?" Katherine asked.

Lavina hesitated for a moment before she said:

"I am rather ... afraid the gowns we ... wear will be very ... expensive and you know ... Papa is not ... well off."

"Of course I know that," Katherine said, "and I would not think of asking your father, whom I have admired since I was a child, to pay for something of which he would most certainly not approve."

"Then who ...?" Lavina began.

"I have not had time to tell you everything," Katherine interrupted, "but one of the girls who is helping me is Suzana Heatherington and she is enormously rich because her mother is American. She has said that she will pay for everything you wear."

"That is very generous," Lavina answered.

She was thinking, however, that it was rather a waste of money.

They would never wear the gowns again.

As if she knew what Lavina was thinking, Katherine said:

"As the gowns will be made up by a really important Dressmaker in London who in fact is known to dress a number of the Gaiety girls, I am sure when the excitement is all over we shall be able to take off some of the frills and furbelows, and use the gowns without them looking over-spectacular."

Lavina thought this was very exciting.

She had bought two new gowns since she had come

out of mourning for her mother.

They were cheap but attractive and, although she did not realise it, she looked lovely in them.

But they would certainly not compete with the sort of gowns which Katherine wore.

"You will meet Suzana when we arrive," Katherine was saying. "She is very pretty, and so is Millicent, who also is staying with us, besides Doris Vincent, whose father is in the Cabinet."

Lavina could not help thinking that it would be a disaster if anyone knew what they were doing.

If the prank got into the newspapers, Doris's father would be very angry.

However, she knew it was no use arguing any further with her friend.

Ever since she was a child Katherine had managed to have her own way.

When they had lessons together it was always Katherine who decided what they should do in their playtime.

Katherine also thought up adventures and parties which made everything seem thrilling for Lavina.

The horses drew up outside Wick House.

It was a very impressive mansion but with no particular architectural quality about it.

It had been added to by several generations.

What had been done fifty years ago had not improved the original building.

It was the same inside, as Lavina knew—a *potpourri* of several centuries mixed together.

Because she had known it for so many years, Lavina loved it.

She felt as she entered the Hall that it was almost like coming home.

In the last months the house had been shut up.

Katherine had been away and she had felt it all looked gloomy.

She hated to see the shutters drawn over the windows and no smoke coming from the chimneys.

The old Butler, who had been at Wick House for years, greeted her respectfully.

"Nice t'see you, Miss Lavina!" he said. "An' I hopes th' Vicar's well?"

"Very well, thank you, Dobson," Lavina replied. "I am sure my father will want to know how your rheumatism is."

"It gives I th' same pains it's always done!" Dobson replied.

He smiled as he spoke and Lavina smiled back at him.

She knew that because of his rheumatism he was unable to go to Church.

It was too far to walk down the long drive into the village.

Katherine was not listening.

She was hurrying ahead to the Sitting-Room she always used when her friends came to stay.

It was known as the "Blue Room."

It was very attractive, but not as large as the Drawing-Room, which was kept for special occasions.

As she opened the door, Lavina could see there were two girls waiting.

They were both, as Katherine had said, extremely pretty.

Lavina was introduced.

Suzana had dark hair and large, flashing eyes which dominated her straight nose and square chin.

Millicent was more slender.

She had a pointed face beneath a cloud of naturally curly fair hair which seemed to have caught the sunshine.

She had an irresistible smile.

It was almost impossible for anyone she smiled at not to smile in return.

"Now, here is Lavina," Katherine said, "and as I have already told you, she is far cleverer than any of us."

"And she is lovely!" Millicent exclaimed. "That is more important than anything else."

"Nonsense," Katherine said. "We are trying to prove that it is not looks that count, but our brains."

The girls laughed and Suzana said:

"If we are pretending to be Gaiety Girls, it is our faces which will be a good introduction."

"That is true enough," Katherine agreed. "How have you got on with the task I set you?"

"Very well," Millicent replied. "Do you want to hear them?"

She had a piece of paper in her hands.

She was just about to read from it when she saw that Lavina was looking curious.

"Katherine told us," she explained, "that we were to work out our names as Gaiety Girls so that we can remember them when the Marquis addresses us."

"I agree that is important," Lavina replied.

She thought that anyway she would be nervous of acting the part that Katherine was giving her.

If she also had to remember she was called by some strange name, it would go out of her head at the last moment.

"Read out what you have chosen," Katherine ordered impatiently.

"I of course will be 'Milly,'" Millicent said, "and I thought 'Milly Mills' would sound theatrical."

"It does," Katherine murmured.

"Elizabeth will be 'Betty Butt,'" Millicent went on. "Doris will be 'Dolly Dalton.'"

"That is rather long," Katherine objected.

Because she thought she ought to explain, she said to Lavina:

"You see, we know that George Edwardes likes his Show-girls to have names which are easy to remember and which sound rather exciting."

"Very well," Suzana said, "she can be 'Dolly Dawes.'"

"That is much better!" Katherine approved.

"And Constance will be 'Connie Corry,'" Millicent continued. "Wendy can keep her Christian name as it is, and be 'Wendy Winn,' Suzana—'Susie Shaw,' and Iris—'Iris Locke.'"

Katherine clapped her hands.

"That is splendid! Now, what about Lavina?"

Lavina drew in her breath.

She was secretly trying to think how her name could be converted into something easy but also rather common.

"I think," Millicent said, "'Vina Vern' would be a splendid name for Lavina."

"Oh, yes," Lavina exclaimed, "I can remember that!"

"It suits you," Millicent said, "and also sounds a bit more intelligent than our names!"

Katherine gave a sigh.

"Well, that is settled!" she said. "I will be Kathy. And now we have to get our gowns. By the way, Rupert told me last night that the Marquis has arranged that his private railway carriage will be attached to the train which leaves Paddington Station at three o'clock on Saturday afternoon."

Lavina looked surprised.

"But surely we are supposed to be performing that evening?"

"You have forgotten what I told you," Katherine replied. "We have been on tour and have just returned to London, so we have nothing to do until we leave again on Monday for the next Town at which we are appearing."

Lavina apologised.

"I had indeed forgotten!"

"That gives us two nights at the house, and we leave very early on Monday morning."

Lavina wanted to say she thought it was too long.

As, however, the others seemed to accept it, she thought it would be a mistake to complain.

"I am going back to London the day after tomorrow," Katherine said, "and Lavina will come with me."

Lavina gave a little cry.

"Do you really mean that?"

"Of course I mean it. You have to fit your gowns, and, of course, you must also see the Show at the Gaiety which is *The Shop Girl*."

Lavina's eyes were shining.

"That will be very exciting for me."

"We shall have to go to a matinée," Katherine said, "otherwise the Marquis might be there. He is not likely to notice us. At the same time, it is not worth the risk."

"No, of course not," Millicent said, "and you can take Lavina alone because the rest of us have seen the Show."

"That is true," Suzana said, "and Lavina can see how we shall have quite a struggle to make ourselves as attractive as the Gaiety Girls."

"It is the Marquis who will have to admit that!" Katherine said grimly.

They sat talking over what they were going to do.

As they did so, Lavina was aware that Katherine was really upset by what the Marquis had said.

'I cannot think why it should worry her,' she wondered.

It suddenly occurred to her that perhaps Katherine, although she had never met him, was in love with the Marquis.

It seemed unlikely.

From what the other girls said, Katherine was such a success and so greatly admired that it seemed rather childish to present one dissenting voice amongst all the others.

But she was thrilled at the idea of going to London.

When Katherine sent her back in the carriage later in the evening she felt as if she were dancing on air.

Her father was still in his Study.

It was getting time for him to change for dinner, so she interrupted him.

He looked up as she entered the room and asked vaguely:

"What is the time?"

"It is seven o'clock, Papa, and time you stopped working. Besides, I have something exciting to tell you."

"What is it?" the Vicar asked.

He was moving his papers so that Lavina knew he was not really concentrating on her answer.

"Katherine has been here to-day," Lavina said, "and she has asked me to go to London with her next week!"

"Katherine?" the Vicar exclaimed.

Then, as if he suddenly remembered who it was, he said:

"Oh, she is home, is she? Well, that is very nice for you, my dear."

"Very nice," Lavina agreed, "and you will not mind me going to London for a few days?"

The Vicar put down his papers and came from behind his desk.

"To be truthful," he said, "I have been a little hurt that Katherine has paid so little attention to you lately. When you were children you used to be so happy together."

"Katherine has apologised for her neglect," Lavina said, "and I do understand. She was having such a busy time in London that she found it difficult to remember the 'Country Bumpkins' who live in Little Wickington."

"And now she has asked you to stay with her," the Vicar said.

"Just for a few days," Lavina said. "Then I might

be invited to a party which is being given by the Marquis of Sherwood."

She wondered, as she spoke, if her father would have heard of the Marquis and perhaps object to her being one of his guests.

But the Vicar merely said:

"That sounds very enjoyable, and I am so glad for you, my dear."

He walked out of the Study, then, as he reached the staircase, he stopped.

"I have just thought," he said, "if you are going to London, you will need some new clothes, and I will spare you everything I can."

"There is no need for you to do that, Papa," Lavina said quickly. "Katherine has already told me I can borrow anything I want from her and she always has far more than she needs."

The Vicar laughed.

"That applies to the whole family! At the same time, they are certainly not mean about their money."

He went up the stairs.

"That reminds me—I want to ask the Earl to do something about the Alms Houses. They really are getting rather shabby!"

"I will ask Katherine to tell me when her father is coming home, but I have the idea that he is enjoying himself in London as much as she is!"

As she spoke, Lavina was thinking that the Earl had in many ways been very lonely since he had been a widower.

Like her father, he was still handsome.

She was certain there would be parties for him

with old friends who would make him happy.

After dinner her father read to Lavina the work he had done on his book during the afternoon.

She thought it very interesting.

She forgot everything else while she listened to him.

He read beautifully in his deep, cultivated voice.

When she listened to him in Church she felt it had an hypnotic quality about it which made even the fidgetty choirboys listen.

Now he was writing about the places he had visited, especially those in the East.

He made her feel as if she could visualise them clearly, so what he was describing was like a picture in front of her.

He was writing about India.

She could see the brilliance of the sun shining on the River Ganges.

There were brilliantly coloured saris lying out to dry.

Then there were the crowds moving down to bathe in the water they believed to be holy, and the canopied boats floating slowly by them on the tide.

As her father finished, she gave a little sigh.

"That was lovely, Papa! You make me feel as if I have actually been to India!"

"I would like to take you there," the Vicar said as he smiled, "but I am afraid it is something we cannot afford."

He sighed.

She knew he was longing to travel all over the world as he had done when he was younger, climbing mountains and sailing up uncharted rivers.

He would love to talk to natives who looked different from the people in Little Wickington.

"Perhaps one day we shall be able to go off on a long holiday," Lavina said aloud. "We must save every penny we can."

For a moment the Vicar's eyes seemed to light up. Then he answered:

"It sounds delightful. At the same time, my dearest, I do not intend to economise on you. If you see some pretty gowns you want to buy in London, you are to buy them. I feel sure when this book is finished I shall get an advance on it from the Publishers."

"That is very sweet of you, Papa," Lavina said, "but I would rather visit Greece than have a new gown."

"We will do both," the Vicar said firmly.

He knew it would be difficult to arrange.

He would have to find somebody to take his place while he was away.

When they went up to bed hand-in-hand, Lavina began to worry in case he would be lonely while she was in London.

Then she told herself that Nanny would look after him.

Besides, until his book was finished, he would be perfectly happy to be alone.

*　　*　　*

The hours seemed to pass slowly while Lavina was waiting to go to London with Katherine.

She tried to think of everything that could be done to make her father comfortable in her absence.

"I shall listen to every Chapter you have written

as soon as I return home," she told him.

"They will be waiting for you," he answered.

He kissed her good-bye, and she waved until the Vicarage was out of sight.

Then, as she sat down beside Katherine, she said:

"Papa is often lonely, as I think your father is sometimes. Mama used to say that a widow could cope better than a widower."

"I am sure that is true," Katherine agreed, "and I am always glad when my father has a flirtation with an attractive woman. At the same time, I know he will never put anybody else in my mother's place."

"I could say the same about Papa," Lavina said, "and I suppose it is the penalty for having been so very happy in their marriages."

She thought as she spoke that that was what she wanted when she married.

She wanted to love a man so much that nothing else in the world mattered, and for him to feel the same about her.

"Have you had any proposals, Katherine?" she asked.

"Two," Katherine replied, "but no one whom Papa would accept as a son-in-law."

Lavina thought for a moment.

Then she asked:

"What would your father do if you fell in love with somebody who, from his viewpoint, was unsuitable?"

"He would prevent me from marrying him, and there would be nothing I could do about it," Katherine replied.

"But suppose you were...in love?" Lavina persisted.

There was silence.

Then Katherine said:

"I hope I will be sensible enough not to fall in love with anyone who could not give me the position in life that I want, or have enough money to provide me with everything I need."

Lavina knew Katherine was saying exactly what she believed was essential for her happiness.

She thought, although she did not say so, that that was not real love.

It was not the love she wanted, and which was part of her dreams.

Living in the country and seeing very few people, especially this last year when she had been in mourning, she knew very little about men, except, of course, what she had read in books.

She imagined the man she loved would be a hero like those in a Walter Scott novel.

Or perhaps he would be strange, cynical, yet unstable like a Jane Austen hero.

He would also be a mixture of the Knights of Chivalry and the explorers, those who ventured into parts of the world where no white man had ever travelled.

He should be brave in being willing to use his life to save a damsel in distress, or a helpless child.

She was sure that the man she loved would be all these things.

One day she would meet him and they would live happily ever after.

* * *

Kenwick House in London was large and, Lavina thought, rather gloomy.

It was, however, comfortable, and there were a great many servants to look after the Earl and his daughter.

"I have a chaperon staying in the house," Katherine told Lavina, "because there has to be somebody there when Papa is away at the Races, or shooting."

"Who is she?" Lavina asked.

"She is a rather tiresome old Cousin who is delighted to come and stay for as long as we want her, but really, on the whole she does not interfere, except that she is a bore."

The way Katherine spoke made Lavina feel rather sorry for the poor relation.

At the same time, she remarked that Katherine had always been impatient with her innumerable Cousins and other relatives who toadied to her father.

The two girls had no sooner arrived at Kenwick House when Millicent appeared and also Suzana.

"We have been longing to tell you," they said, "that we have told the Dressmaker who is making our gowns to come here to-morrow to fit them."

"Here?" Katherine exclaimed.

"Well, you know Mama would be curious about anything I have chosen for myself," Millicent explained, "and Suzana says that her father is already asking awkward questions about where we are staying on the week-end of the twenty-third."

"I hope you told him it would be with me," Katherine said.

"Of course I did," Suzana replied. "But he asked me several times with whom we were going to stay."

"You can always say 'my friends in the country',

or else make up a name," Katherine said. "That is what I intend to tell my father, but not until the last moment."

"It was a mistake for me to tell Papa so soon," Suzana said. "But he was making plans for us to go to a luncheon-party on the Sunday, so I had to say that I would be away."

"For goodness' sake, be careful," Katherine said. "You know relations are always nosey, and somebody might find out the truth. They will not believe for one moment that the Marquis has invited eight *débutantes* to Sherwood Park."

"That is true," Millicent said, "and I promise you, Katherine, I will be very careful."

They made plans about the next day, then left.

Lavina found there was a small dinner-party of the Earl's friends.

She would have put one of her own simple gowns, but Katherine called her into her bed-room and told her to choose from a whole wardrobe filled with beautiful creations.

"Surely you do not want me to wear any of these?" Lavina exclaimed.

"I have had most of them for several months," Katherine said, "and I really hate being seen in any dress more than twice."

Lavina chose a gown that was simpler than the others, but when she had it on it was very becoming.

It was white with touches of pink on it and Katherine gave her a pink rose to wear in her hair.

The guests at dinner were the same age as the Earl.

But there was no doubt they found Lavina very

attractive and paid her compliments that made her blush.

Rupert Wick was also there, and when the meal was over he came down to sit beside her in the Drawing-Room.

"Katherine is delighted you are taking part in her 'Charade,'" he said.

"I . . . I hope I will not . . . make a mess of it," Lavina said humbly.

"I am sure you will not," Rupert replied. "I can tell you, and this is the truth, you are far lovelier than any Gaiety Girl the Marquis has ever escorted, and there have been a large number of them."

"Katherine says he is obsessed by them! Are they really so . . . wonderful?"

Rupert hesitated for a moment before he said:

"They are great fun and far more glamorous than any others of their sort."

Lavina thought he was referring to chorus girls, and she said:

"I have heard so much about them from Katherine that they seem to be more important than any other women in the whole of London!"

"Perhaps you are right," Rupert said as he smiled, "and personally I find them amusing and delightful to be with. It does not matter to me whether or not they have any brains."

Lavina knew he was thinking it rather foolish of Katherine to want to convince the Marquis that *débutantes* were clever.

Then she said a little tentatively:

"Supposing the Marquis is . . . angry with you for . . . deceiving him?"

"As a matter of fact, I have wondered about that," Rupert replied, "but as he is a sportsman, nobody would deny that, I am sure, when he thinks about it he will see the joke and laugh."

Lavina knew that was not how Katherine wanted him to feel.

She knew, however, it would be a mistake to criticise Katherine's plans, and she said nothing.

"Now, do not feel nervous," Rupert said. "All you have to do is smile and look as lovely as you are now, and the Marquis will have to eat his words."

He looked at her admiringly before he added:

"And if he is not bowled over at first sight, I can tell you some of the other guns will be!"

That was at least re-assuring.

When Lavina went to bed she did not feel so frightened about what lay ahead as she had before.

The next day the girls spent a great deal of time fitting on the clothes which the Dressmaker had brought to Kenwick House.

In order to avoid the servants being aware of what was going on, and talking, Katherine sent away her Lady's-Maid.

As they inspected the gowns she locked the door.

Lavina thought them all lovely.

Yet the difference between Katherine's ordinary gowns and those to be worn at the Marquis's party was quite obvious.

The Dressmaker had simply been told they were for some "theatricals" the girls were planning.

"We all have to look very smart, as if we were on the stage of a London Theatre," Katherine had explained.

"Then I know exactly what you want, M'Lady," the Dressmaker answered. "And in fact you'll find these gowns are good enough for the Gaiety!"

"I had heard you have made some gowns for the Gaiety Girls," Katherine said.

"Oh, yes, M'Lady!" the Dressmaker replied, "and several of them have been dressed entirely by us, and of course not only at George Edwardes's expense."

She said the last three words in a low voice.

It was as if she did not want anyone to hear what she said to Katherine.

Lavina, however, was listening.

She wondered exactly what the woman was implying.

Then, intent on her own gown, she forgot everything but the excitement of looking very different from how she had ever appeared in her life before.

When the Dressmaker had gone, Katherine produced a little box for each of the girls.

It contained the special cosmetics they had to use on their faces.

She had bought them from a shop which catered for all kinds of stage make-up.

Opening her box, Lavina found it contained powder, rouge, mascara, and a little brush with which to apply it.

In addition, there were several small powder-puffs.

"Now what you have to do," Katherine said, "is to practice at home. But do be careful not to let anybody see what you are doing, or they will be bound to ask questions. Then, because they will talk, somebody might guess what we are doing."

"We will be very careful," the girls promised.

"It is not going to be easy to get it right at first," Katherine said, "and as Lavina knows, once or twice when we have acted in the Charades at Christmas we have made ourselves look grotesque by wearing too much rouge and making our eyebrows too heavy."

"That is true," Lavina said, "you should be careful not to be too heavy-handed with any of these things."

"At the same time, we want to look theatrical," Katherine said.

"We will practise, of course we will practise!" Constance promised. "And we will also lock our doors."

They left the house, laughing.

They were looking so lovely as they did so that Lavina thought it was a pity the Marquis could not see them as they were now.

She thought differently the day after Katherine had taken her to the Gaiety.

There was a matinée on Wednesdays and Saturdays.

When they drove to the Theatre Lavina thought it was one of the most exciting things that had ever happened to her.

Because she had never been to one before, she was impressed by the entrance.

When they were shown into a Box she looked round and realised that the Theatre was far bigger than she had expected.

The girls were not, of course, allowed to go on their own and had taken Cousin Jane with them.

All the way there she told them rather boringly

of the different Plays she had seen in the past.

"Of course," she said, "Musical Comedy is quite new, but I doubt if they have improved on the delightful entertainments that preceded it."

Katherine was making no pretence at listening to what her Cousin Jane was saying.

Lavina politely tried to sound interested when she paused for breath.

"Who wrote the script for the Play?" she asked Katherine when it was possible to speak.

Katherine looked surprised.

"I never thought of it as having an Author," she replied.

"I expect there is one," Lavina remarked, thinking of her father.

She wished that one of his books could be made into a Play for the Stage.

When they bought a programme, Lavina found that the book of *The Shop Girl* had been written by H. J. W. Donn.

Because it meant nothing to her, she did not realise it was a name new to the Gaiety.

George Edwardes had wanted an Author who was not in any way connected with the tradition of *Burlesque*.

The programme also told her who had composed the music.

The lyrics were written and the whole Show produced by somebody called James Tanner.

She was clever enough, however, to be certain that the most important phrase in the programme was:

Produced under the personal direction of
Mr. George Edwardes

When the curtain rose, Lavina became enthralled and thrilled every minute by the glittering and dazzling Show.

She was enchanted by the Stars—particularly Celia Loftus and Katy Seymour.

But it was the Gaiety Girls who made her draw in her breath.

She in fact thought how presumptuous it was of Katherine and her friends to think they could emulate anything so fascinating.

When the Show-girls were on the stage she felt as if she could hardly breathe.

Only when the final curtain fell amid applause did she feel as if she had come back to reality.

The Gaiety performance had carried her into a dream-world she had never known existed.

* * *

Driving home, she was silent, while Cousin Jane was still talking.

Lavina was thinking she could understand exactly why the Marquis had no wish to spend his time with *débutantes*.

How could he possibly find them interesting when he could be with the goddess-like creatures called the Gaiety Girls?

They might have stepped out of a picture painted by Botticelli or some other great master of the canvas.

For perhaps the first time in her life Lavina thought her friend Katherine was asking too much.

How could anyone, especially herself, compete with the irresistible glamour of the Gaiety?

chapter three

"THE trouble with you," the Earl of Kenwick had said once to his daughter, "is that you have a man's brain. You should have been a boy."

Lavina had been present at the time and she was sure the Earl was right.

Katherine was a born organiser and would have made an excellent Commander of a Regiment.

She thought of every detail.

Lavina admired her more and more as the preparations for their Charade continued.

It was Katherine who decided where they should change.

They had to discard their ordinary clothes and put on those in which they would travel to Sherwood Park.

She went to a House Agent.

She told him that some American friends who were

coming to London for a week disliked staying in Hotels.

Quite a number of society people had gone to the country.

He easily found her an excellent house just off Grosvenor Square.

It was well furnished and the only servants were two old caretakers.

They would not be concerned with what Katherine and her friends were doing and were unlikely to talk to other servants.

"What we have to be careful of," Katherine told the girls when they were assembled, "is first of all our Lady's-Maids, who, of course, will pack for us before we leave, and secondly, the coachman who will drive us to the station."

"Then how are we going to get there?" Suzana asked.

"Rupert will arrange that for us," Katherine said, "but first we have to go to the house I have rented, unpack our trunks, and put into them the clothes which will be waiting for us there."

Lavina thought it was very clever of her to have worked everything out so sensibly.

She knew better than anyone else that the slightest hint of what they were doing would sweep through London.

It would even reach the servants at Wick House.

Doris, who Lavina thought was rather spoilt, said somewhat petulantly:

"I will never be able to manage without a Lady's-Maid!"

"Gaiety Girls are unlikely to have Lady's-Maids,"

Katherine said sharply, "but of course at Sherwood Park a housemaid will look after you personally."

Doris had to be content with this, and Katherine had thought of yet another detail.

It had been very mild for October and, now that they were into November, it was getting cold.

"We shall need furs," she said, "and I do not think the capes and coats we usually wear will be flashy enough."

Suzana laughed.

"I am sure Gaiety Girls have chinchilla, sable, and ermine, and would turn their noses up at anything else."

"That is what I was thinking," Katherine agreed, "so you must all try to borrow something from your mothers or if you cannot do that, I have quite a number of really lovely furs which belonged to mine."

Lavina did not say anything.

She knew that the thick coat she wore in the Winter would certainly not look very glamorous in London.

Although her mother had owned a fur she wore in the evening, it was not a very expensive one.

She had, however, looked lovely in it.

"I have something special for you, Lavina," Katherine said, as if she knew what she was thinking.

When Lavina saw it she thought it was very special indeed.

It was a blue velvet cape which reached almost to her knees.

It was lined with a soft white fur which she did not think was very valuable.

But down the front and round the neck there was a broad band of ermine.

When Lavina tried it on she looked very lovely in it.

"Mama used to wear it to go to the Opera," Katherine said, "but I am sure a Gaiety Girl would wear it for travelling in the Marquis's special railway carriage."

"I will be very, very careful with it," Lavina promised.

"And with my mother's jewellery, I hope!" Katherine laughed.

Lavina looked startled.

"Are we to wear jewellery?"

"Of course!" Katherine answered. "All the Gaiety Girls have jewellery which is worth a lot of money."

Lavina looked puzzled.

"Surely Mr. Edwardes does not provide them with jewels as well as their gowns?"

Katherine laughed.

"They have plenty of admirers to bedeck them like Indian Maharanees!"

As soon as she spoke she realised she had made a mistake.

Since Lavina had come to London she had found how innocent she was.

Katherine had been at a Finishing School, so she and her other friends were much more sophisticated.

They talked about the Gaiety Girls.

Inevitably they had a brother or a cousin who had taken one or more out to supper.

Sooner or later they confided that they had spent money on them.

In one case it had been the girl's father who had made her mother very unhappy because of his attachment to a Gaiety Girl.

Katherine remembered her saying:

"Mama was at first furious when she found out that Papa had given the girl a diamond necklace, then she cried."

Katherine had no intention of imparting this sort of information to Lavina.

She was clever enough to realise that one of the great attractions about her was her innocence and purity.

"As soon as this commotion is over," she told herself, "I will introduce her to some really charming young men and hope she will find a rich husband."

She was still feeling guilty that she had left Lavina for so long without seeing or communicating with her.

"I was very selfish," Katherine told herself, "especially as she has been like a sister to me."

In her own mind she was preparing Lavina to astonish the Social World in which she intended to take her.

She therefore took a great deal of trouble over what she should wear to surprise the Marquis.

One of the prettiest gowns the Dressmaker had brought them was in a very pale blue like the sky on a Spring day.

On Lavina it looked breathtaking.

The colour reflected her eyes and made her skin translucent.

Katherine decided that everything Lavina would wear during the visit should be blue.

Each of the other girls was given a different colour and because Katherine was in command nobody argued.

Suzana looked lovely in green and Doris in lilac.

Millicent had a gown that was black over white which made her appear very dramatic and so *chic* that she might have been French.

"I will borrow my mother's large diamond necklace," she said. "Only for Heaven's sake, do not let me lose it!"

"Are you wise to wear anything so valuable?" Constance asked.

"I can hardly believe the Marquis would steal it!" Millicent laughed. "Mama is going away that weekend and it will be too grand for her to wear in the country."

Nearly all of the Girls managed to bring some sort of spectacular jewellery.

They showed it to each other proudly when they arrived at the house in which they were to change.

Katherine had a large jewel-box with her which contained some of her mother's jewellery.

"I nearly brought the tiara!" she said. "But I thought even the Marquis might think that was overdoing things!"

The girls laughed.

Lavina was thrilled with the necklace of pearls which Katherine had loaned her.

She also produced another of turquoises and diamonds, with ear-rings to match.

The girls arrived at the house off Grosvenor Square one after the other.

On Katherine's instructions they all sent away

the carriages which had brought them there.

Before the coachmen and the footmen left, however, they were ordered to put the trunks in the hall.

They were told they would be collected almost immediately by the vehicles which would convey their owners to where they were spending the week-end.

As soon as the girls were all there Katherine locked the front door.

Then they started to unpack their trunks.

They replaced the clothes with the fantastic gowns which had been left for them that morning.

Lavina quickly did as she was told.

She saw, however, that Katherine's friends had obviously never done their own packing before and she helped them.

Having always looked after herself, it presented no problems for her.

Katherine and those of her friends who had been at a Finishing School had also managed without a Lady's-Maid.

The packing done, they took off their gowns upstairs in the bed-rooms.

They hung them up in the wardrobes.

"We will have to collect them on Monday morning," Katherine said, "and if we leave them lying about, they will be creased."

That was practical advice and most of the girls had not thought of it.

They were all very excited as they changed into the lovely day gowns for which Suzana had paid.

Lavina's was, of course, blue.

With it was a hat trimmed with small ostrich feathers.

It was different from any she had ever worn before.

Before they put on their hats, Katherine told them to make up their faces.

As they had all been practising, they had become quite proficient at it.

When finally Lavina looked at herself in the mirror, she thought it would be difficult even for her father to recognise her.

She certainly looked very lovely.

But she was sure her mother would have shuddered at her red lips and long, dark eye-lashes.

They made her eyes seem much larger than they usually were.

"You look lovely!" Katherine exclaimed when she saw her.

"I am sure no one would recognise me," Lavina said as she laughed.

"I hope we can all say the same," Doris remarked, "and I was very careful not to go to any parties this week where I might have met one of the Marquis's friends who would be shooting with him."

"How could you be sure of that?" Lavina asked.

"Well, for one thing," Doris said, "they would all be about his age and therefore, like him, not interested in *débutantes*."

"What is his age?" Lavina asked.

It was a question she had not thought to ask before.

"I suppose he is about twenty-nine or thirty," Doris replied.

Lavina was surprised.

From the way the others had talked about the Marquis, she had thought he was much older.

"He never bothers himself with younger men,"

Katherine, who had been listening, interrupted, "except for Rupert, and that is because he is such an outstanding rider."

Lavina, having been with Rupert and Katherine since she was small, knew this was true.

In fact, both brother and sister were outstandingly proficient on any horse they mounted.

One thing really had delighted her.

It was that Katherine had told the girls they were all to bring their riding-habits with them.

"I am longing to ride the Marquis's horses!" Millicent cried.

"We may have difficulty in persuading him to let us do so," Katherine replied, "for the simple reason that Rupert tells me few of the Gaiety Girls are any good on a horse and therefore the Marquis would expect us all to be 'Park Trotters'!"

"Then that will be another surprise for His Lordship!" Constance laughed.

Lavina had been worried about her habit, which was getting old, until Katherine said:

"I have a habit for you, Lavina, in which you will look sensational! I have not worn it myself because it is too smart!"

Lavina looked at her questioningly, and she explained:

"Mama and I went to another Tailor instead of Busvine, and it was a mistake. Once the habit was made, Mama told me not to wear it because she thought it was slightly vulgar."

She saw Lavina's face and laughed.

"Not the way you are thinking," she said, "but it accentuates the waist, and is braided round the collar and cuffs, which is distinctly out of place in the hunting-field."

Lavina knew this was true and that ladies' habits were now very severe.

"Thank goodness we wear the same size in boots!" Katherine went on. "Although your feet are a trifle smaller than mine. But the pair I am lending you are brand new and a little tight for me."

Lavina was not listening.

She was thinking that the most exciting thing she could imagine was to be allowed to ride one of the Marquis's superb horses.

Since Katherine had talked about him she had looked for his name in the newspapers.

She found it continually on the sporting pages.

There were innumerable references to his race-horses at Newmarket and the horses in his stables at Sherwood Park.

Another thing she had missed while Katherine had been away had been the rides they had had together.

They had raced each other and dared each other to jump very high fences.

When she looked back, she saw them as having spent all their time when they were young laughing at themselves and everything else.

It had all been such fun.

Now that she was with Katherine again, it seemed to have brought the sunshine back into her life.

"Are we all ready?" Katherine asked when they had put on their hats and the furs in which they were to travel.

Katherine herself had a magnificent stole of sable

and a huge muff to match it.

The other girls were nearly as smart.

Lavina thought nothing was more spectacular than her velvet and ermine cape.

"From the moment we leave this room," Katherine instructed, "we cease to have any identity except that of the part we are to play."

The girls murmured and Katherine went on:

"You must be very careful to use the names you have chosen for yourselves. Remember, we have all been on tour in *The Girl* in Birmingham, and expect to be going to Manchester on Monday."

She paused before she added:

"Talk as little about the Theatrical World as possible, but stun His Lordship with your other interests. You all have them, and you must contrive somehow to show off your talents this evening and to-morrow."

When she had finished talking, the girls laughed.

Katherine opened the door and started to walk down the stairs.

Lavina followed her and saw that Rupert was waiting for them in the hall.

He was standing amongst their luggage and looking, she thought, very smart.

"We are ready, Rupert," Katherine said. "Are the carriages here?"

"Waiting outside," Rupert confirmed. "Shall I tell the men to collect these?"

He made a gesture with his hand and Katherine replied:

"Yes, please do."

Rupert opened the front-door.

The trunks were carried out and placed in the third carriage, in which no one was travelling.

They divided themselves into two groups, Rupert travelling with Katherine, Lavina, and Millicent.

"I must say," he remarked as the horses drove off, "you all look absolutely stunning!"

His eyes were on Lavina as he spoke.

When she saw the expression in them she blushed.

"I have to admit, Katherine," he added, "that when you have one of your bright ideas, you really do it well!"

"It is Kathy!" his sister corrected him. "We must all be very careful to address each other by our 'Gaiety Girl' names."

"Of course," Rupert replied. "I am sorry, I forgot, and can I tell 'Vina' that if she was on the stage of the Gaiety, she would stop the Show!"

"Now you are making me jealous!" Millicent complained.

She spoke lightly.

The way she looked at Rupert made Lavina suspect that she found him very attractive.

He had turned round as she spoke.

Now he took her hand and raised it to his lips.

"I have told you a thousand times how beautiful I think you are!" he said. "But you never listen to me!"

"Well, I will be listening this week-end," Millicent promised, "and I hope you will look after me. I do not want to get into trouble with the Marquis's friends. After all, we are pretending to be Gaiety Girls, so you know what they will expect."

Lavina, who was listening, looked puzzled, and Katherine said quickly:

"There will be no difficulties of that sort because I have told you all to be careful and lock your doors. If that is a surprise in itself—all the better!"

"Why should we do that?" Lavina enquired.

There was a little pause before Katherine said lightly:

"You know this is an unchaperoned party and if some of the men have too much to drink they might behave in a riotous manner."

"You do not ... think they might ... come into our bed-rooms?" Lavina asked in a shocked voice.

"When they start ragging about, they might play a joke on you or something like that, so lock your door and do not think about it."

She glanced at her brother as she spoke, and Rupert said:

"Kathy's right. You do not want to be disturbed once you have gone to sleep."

"No ... of course not," Lavina agreed.

She did not see the warning glances that Katherine gave to Millicent, who was about to say something.

She merely thought, as she had thought before, that her mother would not approve.

She would never even think of staying in a bachelor's house without a proper chaperone.

It was, however, too late to think of anything but the instructions that Katherine had given them.

When they arrived at Paddington Station, Rupert escorted them to the train.

He ordered a number of porters to bring their luggage.

Lavina had never been in a private carriage before.

The Marquis's was certainly very impressive.

It was at the end of the train, and three Stewards wearing the Sherwood livery were there to attend to them.

The carriage had very comfortable seats.

They were thickly padded and covered in crimson velvet.

Almost as soon as they sat down Stewards brought them champagne, pâté sandwiches, and some delicious sweetmeats.

Lavina enjoyed everything, including the journey.

She had very seldom been in a train.

Certainly when she had travelled in one with her father she had not been as comfortable as she was now.

Because the girls were all excited at what they were to do, they were laughing all the way until the train stopped.

This was at a small platform on which was written in large letters:

HALT FOR SHERWOOD PARK

The Marquis's carriage was positioned exactly in the centre of the platform on which was laid a red carpet.

There was a senior Servant to meet them.

Two very smart carriages, each drawn by two

horses, were waiting for the guests as well as a Brake for their luggage.

They drove off, sitting as they had before, with Katherine, Millicent, Lavina, and Rupert in the first carriage.

As they did so, Millicent said jokingly:

"Now the curtain is going up and the Play begins!"

"Do not forget there are two acts," Katherine warned, "to-day and to-morrow, and I think I will murder anybody who forgets their lines!"

"Oh, come on!" Rupert said. "You are taking this all too seriously! The whole thing is a joke, and it might be a good idea to tell the Marquis he has been 'had' to-morrow instead of leaving me to do the dirty work after you have gone!"

"You are not to alter the script!" Katherine cried. "We will see it through to the end and only when we have gone will he know the truth."

Lavina thought this was quite right.

It would be embarrassing if they suddenly told the Marquis while they were there that he had been deceived.

Whatever Rupert might think, she was sure he would be very angry.

She had no wish to be involved in a scene.

Because Katherine had spoken so sharply, Rupert shrugged his shoulders.

"All right," he said, "there is no need to snap my head off. I have said I will do what you want, and you must say I have carried out my part of the bargain up until now."

"Of course you have," Katherine said in a different tone of voice, "and I am very grateful, but you know as well as I do that if anything goes wrong, we will all be in serious trouble with our parents."

Rupert nodded.

"Yes, I know that, and you can trust His Lordship to behave like a Gentleman and not to 'spill the beans,' so to speak."

"If he does that," Millicent said, "Papa will not only be angry with me but with him!"

"I have told you no one will ever know what we have done," Katherine said firmly, "and all Rupert has to do is to carry out my instructions."

"All right, all right!" Rupert said testily. "I have promised that is what I will do, so stop nagging!"

Katherine leaned across to pat him on the knee.

"You are not to be cross with me," she said. "You know you have been splendid up until now, and we are bound to be a little on edge to start with just in case the first act does not run as smoothly as it should."

Rupert smiled.

"Remember the old adage: 'It will be all right on the night!' And I am certain it will."

"Cross your fingers," Millicent cried. "I am crossing mine and I am wearing my lucky charm."

She held up her wrist as she spoke.

Lavina saw she was wearing a little coin on a gold chain.

"What is it?" she asked curiously.

"It was given to me by my Godfather when I was Christened," Millicent replied. "It is a fourpenny piece which has been dipped in gold."

"A fourpenny piece?" Katherine exclaimed in surprise.

"He picked it up when he was a young man and was very poor with no prospects."

"And it brought him luck?" Lavina asked.

"He said the luck it brought him was fantastic! From that moment everything went right and eventually—quite by chance—after two unexpected deaths he became Lord Stewart with a large estate and a great fortune!"

"What a wonderful story!" Katherine exclaimed. "Of course it will bring you luck, and you will marry a Royal Prince or at least a Millionaire!"

"I hope you are right," Millicent said, "but so far the applicants for the position have been few and far between!"

She glanced at Rupert as she spoke, but he was looking at the charm.

Lavina could not help thinking that even if she was in love with him, she would not be allowed to marry him.

Rupert was only the younger son.

He therefore had no chance of coming into the title, and Millicent was the daughter of a Duke.

She remembered what Katherine had said.

She was certain Millicent's father would not think Rupert an acceptable son-in-law, whatever Millicent might feel about him.

"The Social standards are all quite wrong," she told herself.

But she knew there was nothing she could do about them.

*　　*　　*

A quarter-of-an-hour later they had their first glimpse of Sherwood Park.

As she looked at it, Lavina thought it was the most beautiful house she had ever imagined.

It was very large, far larger than she had expected.

She knew without asking that it had been designed in the middle of the last century by the Adam brothers.

Her father had taught her quite a lot about architecture.

She appreciated the huge centre block with urns and statues on its roof, which were silhouetted against the sky.

There was a wing on either side of it.

In front of the house was a lake, and they crossed a very beautiful bridge to reach the Courtyard.

Because they were apprehensive, no one in the carriage spoke as the horses came to a standstill.

It was outside a long flight of steps covered with a red carpet.

There were footmen in elaborate livery to open the carriage doors.

A Butler with white hair was waiting in the doorway.

He bowed politely to Rupert, who had stayed in the house before.

When the Girls from the other carriage joined them, footmen came forward to take their cloaks.

While they were being relieved of their furs, Lavina had a chance to look around.

The Hall was very impressive.

There were alcoves which all held statues that Lavina thought were Greek.

A curved and exquisitely carved staircase led up to the floor above.

The Butler led them to the far end of the Hall, where there were double doors.

Opening them both, he announced:

"The Honourable Rupert Wick, M'Lord, and the ladies from London."

This, Lavina thought, was when the Play began.

For a moment she could see only the beauty of the room into which they walked.

It was not a Drawing-Room, as she might have expected.

It was a comfortable Study or Library which she knew would have been the delight of her father.

There were magnificent pictures of horses and a great number of books.

The furniture was all designed for comfort.

There was a deep sofa and armchairs in which a man could relax after enjoying one sport or another.

It was obvious that the men who rose to their feet as they approached had been shooting.

One man detached himself from the rest and came towards them.

Lavina knew she was seeing the formidable Marquis.

It would have been impossible not to know who he was even in a large crowd.

Exceedingly good-looking, tall, and broad-shouldered, she could understand why people were in awe of him.

He had an authoritative air about him, something

which made him different from men like Rupert.

Then she told herself she was being influenced by what she had heard rather than believing the evidence of her own eyes.

"Here we are!" Rupert was saying unnecessarily. "Now let me introduce you to your guests."

There was just a faint pause before he said:

"This is Milly Mills, who I need not tell you is a great success in *The Girl*."

"I am delighted to welcome you to Sherwood Park," the Marquis said as he shook hands with Millicent.

Rupert introduced his sister as "Kathy," Doris as "Dolly," Suzana as "Susie."

Then it was Lavina's turn.

"This is Vina Verne," Rupert said.

Lavina held out her hand and the Marquis took it.

His handshake was like himself—forceful.

She thought, although it was absurd, that there was a strange vibration from his fingers.

It was not what she had expected.

She had listened to Katherine saying he was spoilt, over-conscious of his own importance, and had believed her.

She had also thought perhaps Katherine was right.

It was ridiculous for a man of his age to be obsessed by the Girls from the Gaiety.

Yet, as she watched him greeting the others, Lavina knew he had something which Katherine had missed.

That was a strong, almost over-whelming personality.

Having greeted the new arrivals, the Marquis then introduced the men with him.

They were all as Rupert had said, about his own age or a little older.

Each one might have been portrayed by an Artist as "The Perfect Gentleman."

There was champagne for everybody to drink.

Lavina, having had a glass on the train, took only a few sips of hers.

At home she had not been used to drinking anything except on Christmas Day and birthdays.

She did not wish to blunt in any way the keenness of her brain.

She was afraid of making a mistake, which would anger Katherine.

As soon as they had had something to drink, the Marquis suggested they might like to go upstairs.

"I am sure you would like to rest before dinner," he said.

"That is a good idea," Katherine agreed, "although we are certainly not exhausted after our train journey. We must thank Your Lordship for providing us with such a delightful way in which to travel."

The Marquis smiled.

"I am glad you appreciate my new coach."

"Is it new?" Katherine asked. "I certainly thought it was very elegant!"

"And what was your impression?" the Marquis asked.

He turned to Lavina as he spoke.

As she was not expecting him to notice her, she gave a little start.

"I . . . I was very impressed . . . My Lord," she said,

"and even more impressed by your beautiful house which I know was designed by the Adam brothers."

"Did Rupert tell you that?" the Marquis asked.

"No, but I hope I would recognise their particular style without anyone helping me," Lavina replied.

There was the suspicion of a smile on the Marquis's lips.

As she turned to walk towards the door, Lavina knew that Katherine was pleased with her.

The Housekeeper in rustling black silk was at the top of the stairs.

She escorted them to their rooms on the First Floor.

The house was certainly very impressive.

A maid was already unpacking her trunk and shaking out her gowns before they were hung up in the wardrobe.

The Housekeeper took Katherine farther along the corridor, and the other girls followed her.

Lavina went to the window to look out at the garden.

It sloped down to the lake on the other side of which was a great Park.

She could see spotted deer moving about under the trees.

It was now dusk and she knew it would soon be dark except for the stars in the sky and perhaps a moon.

It was all so beautiful, so exactly what she had longed to see.

But she had only read about such houses in the books in her father's Library.

Her mother, when she was a girl, had stayed in

some of the more important English houses like this.

"I am sure Mama would like me to be here," Lavina said in her heart.

At the same time, she knew her mother would be shocked at what she was doing, certainly at the way in which she had painted her face.

She lay down for a short time, then the housemaids brought in her bath which they arranged in front of the fire.

They poured in hot and cold water from large brass cans and scented the bath with Oil of Violets.

A Turkish towel was put in front of the fire to warm it before she dried herself.

It was all something she had read about, but thought would never happen to her.

Before putting on her gown she sat at the dressing-table to touch up her face, her eyes, and her lips.

One of the maids skilfully arranged her hair.

She was nearly ready when a huge tray of flowers was brought to her door.

Lavina knew that this was a custom in many big houses.

She had, however, never expected to see it for herself.

There were so many flowers to choose from that she hesitated.

The maid, however, said:

"I think them orchids would suit you best, Miss, if you wears them at the back of your 'ead."

As she spoke she picked up a bunch of small star orchids which Lavina saw were very lovely.

"Thank you," she said.

The tray was taken away.

The maid affixed the orchids as she had suggested at the back of Lavina's head.

She thought it was just the touch needed to make her look more sophisticated.

Katherine had insisted that she wear the blue gown.

"First impressions are important," she had said.

It was certainly very dramatic with frills of blue chiffon swirling out over her feet to make a small train behind her.

It was also, Lavina thought, a little too low in the *décolletage*.

Katherine had, however, insisted that that would be expected of a Gaiety Girl.

She felt it looked a little less immodest once she had put on the turquoise and diamond necklace.

It was what Katherine had lent her, and she screwed the ear-rings to the lobes of her ears.

"You looks lovely, Miss!" the maid said admiringly. "I wishes I could see you on the stage!"

"Perhaps you will one day if you come to London," Lavina answered.

"That's wot I 'opes to do," the maid answered, "an' we've 'eard all about 'Is Lordship, watchin' you from 'is Box an' takin' you Ladies out to supper at Romano's. A real 'Dasher'—that's wot 'e is—an' we all admires 'im!"

"Dasher" was a word Lavina had not heard before, but she thought it was very descriptive.

There was a knock on the door, and Katherine came in.

She looked overwhelmingly lovely in a pink gown

with feathers fluttering round her shoulders and a very full skirt.

With it she wore a necklace of drop diamonds which matched the brooch on her bodice and her earrings.

Lavina had not seen her gown before, and she gave a little gasp.

"You look marvellous, Katherine!" she exclaimed admiringly.

"So do you," Katherine answered. "Come along, it would be a mistake to be late for dinner."

They went down the stairs side by side.

They were shown by the Butler into the huge Drawing-Room.

There were three crystal chandeliers alight with candles and the room was massed with flowers.

'This really is like being in Fairy-Land!' Lavina said to herself.

It was then she caught sight of the Marquis.

He was wearing evening dress, and she knew undoubtedly that he was Prince Charming.

chapter four

LAVINA looked round the Dining-Room.

She thought it was the most beautiful room she had ever seen.

It was of Adam's green picked out in white and gold.

The marble mantelpiece was exquisitely sculpted with Greek maidens holding up the shelf.

The silver glittered on the table and she thought no one could look more attractive or more exciting than Katherine and the other girls.

To her surprise, the Marquis, who had arranged the seating, had put Millicent on his right and her on his left.

Lavina smiled a little to herself at his choice of Millicent.

Being a Duke's daughter, she would have sat there by right if he had known who she really was.

It was astonishing that he should have chosen her to sit on his left.

She did not realise that the contrast between Millicent's sophistication and her innocence was very intriguing.

As Katherine had told them to do, the girls all talked vivaciously but on interesting subjects.

They appeared to be amusing their partners at the table.

The Marquis talked first to Millicent.

Lavina was looking up at a picture over the mantelpiece when he said:

"I think, Vina, you are admiring my room."

"It is absolutely beautiful!" Lavina said, "and I was, in fact, admiring the magnificent Van Dyke over the mantelpiece. I am sure he is one of your relations."

"How do you know it is a Van Dyke?" the Marquis enquired.

Lavina smiled.

"I am sure I am not mistaken in seeing that the hands are painted in a brilliant way which Van Dyke made particularly his own."

The Marquis was surprised, but he did not say anything.

He merely asked:

"And what else do you think is of particular interest in the room?"

Lavina looked around her.

"I admire everything," she said. "I am sure the table is Regency and must have been made at the time the Prince Regent took the cloths off at Carlton House and set the fashion for polished tables."

The Marquis thought to himself that somebody must have told her to say this to him.

As she looked so young and, according to Rupert Wick, had not been in London but the Provinces, he could not imagine who it could be.

He had never before met a Gaiety Girl who showed any interest in decoration or furnishings, let alone who had a knowledge of them.

"You are right," he said, "and do you admire my silver?"

"Of course I do," Lavina answered.

"And what period do you think it belongs to?" the Marquis enquired.

Lavina hesitated.

"I may be mistaken," she said a little humbly, "but I think it is either George II or else George III."

"Why do you think that?"

"Because it is plain," she said, "and from what I have read and seen illustrated, silver for the table did not become elaborate until George IV was Prince of Wales."

"You are right," the Marquis agreed, "but why, admiring as you do houses like mine, have you chosen your particular profession? Please tell me about it."

Lavina shook her head.

"I would much rather go on talking about this beautiful house," she said, "and I am only so frightened that I shall not be able to see *all* of it before I have to leave."

The Marquis laughed.

"I will make sure that you see it all."

"Thank you," Lavina said. "I was thinking as I

came down the stairs that it was like stepping into a Fairy-Tale."

"If that is true," the Marquis said, "then of course I must make whatever you wish come true."

Lavina did not say anything, and he went on:

"Surely there is something you want more than anything else? Now, as I wave my magic wand, you must tell me what it is."

Lavina laughed.

"What I wish for is something that is quite impossible ever to obtain, and the most kindly Fairy Godmother could not grant it to me."

"That is a challenge," the Marquis replied, "and as I am of course your Fairy Godfather, I must make sure that you obtain your wish however difficult it may be."

"I told you, it is impossible."

"I like to think that nothing is impossible where I am concerned," he said.

He was wondering as he spoke what she could possibly want and thinking the answer would be very expensive.

At the same time, he was intrigued that she had not immediately answered his question.

"I am waiting," he said after a moment.

"Very well... but I have told you that my wish is impossible to fulfil. It is that I could go to Tibet."

The Marquis stared at her.

"Did you say—Tibet?" he asked.

"I have just been reading the most wonderful and exciting book on the subject," Lavina said. "It is called *Lhasa in Disguise*."

She did not wait for the Marquis to speak, but went on in a rapt little voice:

"The tale is told so sincerely and brilliantly that I felt as if I were walking over every inch of the land the writer described."

She drew in her breath before she continued:

"I saw the Monasteries built on the sides of mountains, the monks in their yellow robes, the pilgrims climbing painstakingly up the rocky paths. Then—"

She paused for a moment, as if it were difficult to describe what she felt.

"Then I reached Lhasa, saw the Potala and actually caught a glimpse of the Dalai Lama!"

Now there was a reverence in her voice.

The Marquis knew that what she was seeing was not an act but something which meant a great deal to her.

After a moment's silence he said quietly:

"You were right, Vina, it would be impossible for you to go to Tibet, but you have obviously been there in your imagination."

"It is the way I have travelled all over the world," she replied, "especially to the places where Papa has been."

She spoke without thinking, then wondered if that was something she should not have said.

"What does your father do?" the Marquis asked.

"He is writing a book," Lavina answered.

She knew she must not say that her father had written several, in case by some unexpected coincidence the Marquis had read one of them.

She thought it was unlikely.

At the same time, Katherine would be very angry if she made a mistake.

Then the Marquis might become suspicious that she was not what she pretended to be.

"I suppose," he was saying, "your father reads to you what he has written, and that is why it seems so real."

"Yes, that is true," Lavina agreed. "And because he reads so well, he paints me a picture that I can see very clearly."

"And what is he writing about at the moment?"

Lavina thought there was nothing wrong in telling him the truth.

"About India," she answered.

"Then I am sure you must find it very interesting," the Marquis said. "I have just been in India myself and I found it fascinating."

"Oh, do tell me where you went," Lavina begged. "Did you see the Ganges?"

"I did!"

"And you saw the pilgrims going down to bathe and believing they were specially blessed?"

"I saw that!"

"You are so lucky!" Lavina said. "But I think I would enjoy most of all to go to Sārnāth, where the Lord Buddha preached his first sermon."

There was a short pause before the Marquis said:

"Is that near Benares? I do not remember it."

"It is the deer park, and whoever was with you should have taken you there. Papa said he found there a wonderful sense of peace. It was difficult to describe, but he said that because the Lord Buddha himself had been there, the vibrations of faith he had evoked still remained and it was impossible not to be aware of them."

Now the Marquis was obviously so surprised at the way Lavina was talking that he could only stare at her.

He was thinking she was certainly the most unusual Gaiety Girl he had ever encountered.

Because he did not speak, Lavina was suddenly afraid she had said something wrong.

"Please, go on telling me what you enjoyed in India," she said. "I am sure you must have stayed with the Viceroy and that must have been very exciting."

"I would rather hear what your father found in India," the Marquis said.

"I will send you his book as soon as it is published," Lavina promised quickly.

She was saved from saying anymore because Millicent attracted the Marquis's attention.

She wanted him to solve a problem between her and the man on her other side.

He had said that the Derby two years ago had been won by a horse called Jupiter.

She was quite certain it was one called Swift.

"Milly is right, George," the Marquis said, "so you must either apologise or pay a forfeit for your ignorance!"

"I am sure a forfeit will be far more acceptable," his friend replied with a slight twist of his lips.

He then told Millicent that when they returned to London he would take her to Bond Street.

She could choose something she really wanted.

Lavina was surprised when she heard Millicent accept his suggestion.

Then she realised that of course when they left
Sherwood Park the Gentlemen whom they had met
there would never find them again.

She wanted to laugh at the idea of these very smart
and aristocratic men looking for eight Gaiety Girls
who had disappeared into thin air.

"What is amusing you, Vina?" the Marquis asked
unexpectedly.

"If I was smiling," Lavina answered, "it is because
I am so happy. It is wonderful being here and seeing
all your beautiful possessions and hearing you talk
of India. It is something I shall always remember."

"You are speaking as if it will not happen again,"
the Marquis said, "but I have a feeling this is the
beginning of a book, not the end!"

Lavina laughed.

"I hope that is true, but perhaps like Fairy-Gold,
if we touch it with human hands, it will vanish."

"If you are suggesting that is what you will do,"
the Marquis replied, "I shall take steps to ensure
that it does not happen."

"How will you do that?" Lavina asked. "Like a
Fairy-Story I can fly away on a magic carpet or use
my wings."

"If we are in a Fairy-Story," the Marquis retorted,
"I shall charm out of a bottle a *Genii* who will track
you down wherever you go and bring you back to me
either on your magic carpet, or perhaps on the back
of a dolphin."

Lavina clasped her hands together.

"You know that Apollo did that! I have often wondered if men ever read the same stories that I read

as a child and thought because they were so thrilling that they were real."

"They were real to me," the Marquis said. "But I have never met anybody . . . before who believed in them."

He thought as he spoke that this was a very strange conversation.

It was certainly something he had not expected to-night.

He had imagined, as had happened before, that his friends and the Gaiety Girls would drink a great deal.

By this time their voices and laughter would be ringing out.

There would be a noise in the room which was very different from what was actually happening this evening.

He looked down the table.

There was no doubt that his friends were intrigued by the beautiful young women who sat with them.

At the same time, they were talking much more seriously, also very much more quietly than had ever happened before at this sort of party.

He had thought when the Gaiety Girls arrived that Rupert Wick had not exaggerated.

He had promised they would be both beautiful and original.

It was certainly true.

In all his experience of the Gaiety, the girls sitting round his table outshone any he had met previously.

He wondered what it was that made them so different.

George Edwardes must have found fresh hunting

grounds for the Girls in his new show, he thought.

"I must remember to ask him about it," the Marquis told himself.

He started to talk to Lavina again to prevent her from being monopolised by the man on her other side.

Because Millicent was sitting on the Marquis's right, it was she who said when dinner was finished:

"I think, My Lord, the Ladies should now leave the Gentlemen to their port."

This again was unusual.

By the time dinner was finished, the Gaiety Girls were usually clinging to the men with whom they had been flirting.

The social rule was therefore broken by their staying on while the port was going round the table.

The Marquis, however, did not argue.

"Yes, of course, if that is what you wish."

Millicent rose to her feet and the other girls got to theirs.

They swept from the room, moving in their elaborate gowns like a collection of humming birds.

As the door closed and the Marquis sat down again, he said:

"I congratulate you, Rupert! You have certainly produced a unique collection of Beauties!"

"I am glad you are not disappointed," Rupert replied.

The Gentlemen moved up the table to be nearer the Marquis.

"I find them astonishing!" a man said who had sat next to Katherine. "I had one of the most interesting conversations I have enjoyed in a long time, and it is something I never expected to happen with any Gaiety Girls!"

One or two of the other men said the same thing.

Although the Marquis did not comment, he was thinking that Vina was certainly unusual.

He could hardly believe her preoccupation with Tibet.

"It must be an act!" he told himself. "No Gaiety Girl of that age could be interested in an obscure country which has closed its borders to everybody from the Western World!"

His guests were still exchanging comments about the Girls they had partnered at dinner.

Sooner than usual he suggested they should join the Ladies and said:

"As we are all tired to-night, I have not arranged anything special, but I expect the Girls will have some idea of what they want to do."

He was aware that one or two of his friends exchanged meaningful glances.

It was what he expected and in fact the real reason for the party.

As they neared the Drawing-Room, the Marquis could hear music being played on the piano.

He realised that the pianist was very gifted.

As he walked in he saw it was the Girl called Betty, who was extremely pretty.

Before he opened the door the music she was playing was a Chopin Étude.

As soon as the gentlemen appeared, she changed it to one of Johann Strauss's lilting tunes that kept all Vienna dancing.

One or two of the Girls who had been reclining on

the sofas rose and moved towards the men.

The man who had sat next to Betty joined her at the piano.

He sat on the stool beside her, talking to her while she played.

Milly was quickly monopolised by the man who had sat on her right.

The Marquis found himself face-to-face with Lavina.

"What would you like to do?" he asked.

She looked up at him with a question in her eyes and he said:

"I know the answer to that. You want to see more of my treasures."

"I would love to do that, but not if it is something that would bore you."

"I never allow myself to be bored," the Marquis replied, "so we will start with my pictures."

He took her to the end of the Drawing-Room.

He was astonished when she recognised a number of pictures on the walls.

Yet she could have read the names of the Artists beneath them.

They moved from the Drawing-Room into an Ante-Room.

In it there was a Rembrandt and a Rubens which particularly thrilled Lavina.

There was a case containing a number of snuff-boxes including some made by Fabergé.

The Marquis had brought them back with him from Russia.

"So you have been to Russia!" Lavina enquired. "How lucky you are!"

"I stayed in St. Petersburg with the Tsar," the Marquis said, "but I did not enjoy myself very much."

"Why not?"

"It is a country of great contrasts, terrible poverty, and wild, unnecessary extravagance."

"I am sure you thought the Serfs were harshly treated," Lavina said. "I have read about them, and could not believe that people who considered themselves civilised could behave in such a heartless manner!"

They talked about Russia, again in a serious way, which the Marquis found surprising.

Unexpectedly, almost as if he were testing her, he said:

"There is something I want to show you. It is in my Study because I have not yet made up my mind where to put it."

They walked from the Ante-Room into where he had been when the Girls arrived.

The Marquis walked over to a cabinet and took something from the lower shelf.

He carried it to Lavina, who was standing in front of the fire.

As the Marquis joined her she saw that he had in his hand a rough box.

It was made of a wood which she was sure did not exist in England.

He opened it, and she saw there was something wrapped in paper inside.

"I have not looked at this or done anything about it since I came back from India," he said, "but I was told it was unique, and I should be interested, Vina, to know what you think about it."

He thought as he spoke that he was behaving rather strangely.

He had never shown this to any of his friends. Why now should he be showing it to a Gaiety Girl?

He took out what was in the box which he threw down on a chair, then unwrapped the paper.

Lavina had no idea what to expect.

But she saw an object in his hands that was deep green in colour.

He held it up for her inspection.

She saw, although it seemed impossible, it was a huge emerald carved in the shape of the Buddha.

She stared at it in disbelief, and the Marquis said:

"I was told it came from Tibet."

She reached out both her hands to take it from him.

As she felt the stone against her skin she looked down at the face of the Buddha.

She knew that what she held was something so precious, and in a way so miraculous, she could not believe it was true.

She could only stare at what she held.

It seemed to her that when the Marquis spoke, his voice came from a long way away.

"What do you make of it?" he asked.

For a moment she could not speak.

Then at last she said:

"You must be...aware that...this is...Holy! It is...something so...precious, so...wonderful that it can...only have come from...a Monastery."

"That is what I thought myself," the Marquis said.

"It is very, very...old," Lavina went on, "and I can feel the...prayers and the faith that has been . . . poured into it . . . vibrating . . . towards me, so I . . . I know I should be kneeling in front of it."

She spoke slowly and quietly, as if in a dream.

Then she asked:

"How could you possibly have come by anything so marvellous?"

"It was when I was in the North of India," the Marquis explained. "A man approached me and said he had something unique he wanted to sell. I was about to leave on the Viceroy's train for Calcutta, so I told him I was not interested. But he persisted, and finally unwrapped the object he was holding having taken it from its box—which is the one I brought home."

"How could you have hesitated once you had seen it?" Lavina asked.

As she spoke she put the Buddha down on a table which stood beside the fireplace.

There was a wall-light just above it which illuminated the emerald so that it glowed.

It was then the Marquis realised that, as she stood looking at the Buddha, Lavina, as if instinctively, put her hands together palm to palm.

It was the age-old attitude of prayer which was also "*Namaste,*" the Indians' way of both greeting a superior being and paying homage to their Gods.

As he looked at her he realised that she was not posing or showing off to him.

With her eyes on the Buddha she was praying.

He just watched her until she said very softly:

"You will . . . have to . . . send this . . . back."

"What do you mean by that?"

"Those to whom it . . . belongs are looking for it. I

am certain it was stolen, and to them it is a terrible and unspeakable loss."

"How can you possibly believe that?" the Marquis asked.

"I just... know it! I feel... as if it... is speaking to me."

She moved away from the table, and sat down in a chair on the other side of the fireplace.

It was, the Marquis thought, as if what she was feeling left her too exhausted to stand.

After a moment, still with her eyes on the Buddha, she said:

"I am sure... this came from one of the... great Monasteries in Tibet and is their most... precious possession."

"Why should you think that?" the Marquis asked.

He wondered at the way her mind was working, but in fact it was something of which he himself had thought.

"I expect you know that in Tibet every house has a small altar to which the whole family prays," Lavina answered, "usually in the morning and in the evening."

"I have heard that," the Marquis acknowledged. "Go on!"

"There is a story I read, which I thought was very revealing, of a Tibetan woman who asked her son who was going to Lhasa if he would bring her back a holy relic."

"I should imagine he found that quite easy!" the Marquis remarked.

"He promised he would do so," Lavina went on, "but he forgot. The next year he went again and promised he would bring something back, but forgot that time. The third year he remembered it just as he was returning home."

"Without, of course, the relic."

The Marquis spoke lightly, as if he did not wish to be serious about what he had shown to Lavina.

"He had forgotten, so he picked up the jawbone of an ass and broke off one of the teeth," Lavina answered. "He gave it to his mother and told her it was a holy relic."

"She believed him?"

"She placed it in the Temple and prayed to it. Other people who lived nearby came and prayed to it too. After a little time the tooth exuded—a blue light."

Lavina spoke simply, her eyes not on him but on the Buddha.

After a moment the Marquis asked:

"Is that what you are seeing?"

"It is what I am ... feeling," Lavina replied. "A vibration that is so strong that I know that this Buddha has performed many ... miracles."

She spoke with such sincerity that the Marquis felt as if they should be in Church.

Because he thought it was out of keeping with what he had planned for the evening, he picked up the Buddha.

He wrapped it in the paper and put it back in the box.

Only as he shut down the lid did Lavina say:

"I think ... that is ... wrong."

"What is?" the Marquis asked.

"To shut the Lord Buddha away. You should have

him near you, perhaps in your bed-room, so that he can watch over...you and you can also...pray to him."

The Marquis determinedly put the box back into the cabinet from which he had taken it.

He shut the glass door.

"You are making me feel that what I possess is creepy," he said, "but I am not sure I believe what you are telling me."

"Why should...you?" Lavina answered, "but actually, I am...sure it is the...truth."

The Marquis wanted to say that he was tired of talking about the Buddha and he wanted to talk about her.

She rose from the chair in which she had been sitting.

Her full skirt fell from her tiny waist and rippled over her feet.

She looked lovely and, the Marquis thought, very desirable.

At the same time, because of what they had been discussing, there was something spiritual about her.

He knew that with any other Gaiety Girl with whom he was alone in his Study, he would by now have taken her in his arms.

He would be kissing her.

He was, however, aware that Lavina's eyes were on the cabinet in which he had shut away the Buddha.

She was not thinking of him.

The Marquis was not only very fastidious, he also never "jumped his fences" too hurriedly.

He walked towards the door.

"Shall we join the others?" he asked.

It was a moment before Lavina answered him.

He knew she had to bring herself back to reality.

She followed him to the door.

As they stepped out of the Study and into the corridor she said:

"It is getting...late and I am rather...tired. I wonder if I could...go to bed?"

He knew she was really so spiritually moved by what she had felt that she did not want to be with a lot of people.

"Of course," he answered. "It would be a mistake to be late to-night. I think everybody has had a long day."

Lavina hesitated, then asked a little tentatively:

"Will we be...able to...ride to-morrow and if so...how early?"

"You wish to ride?" the Marquis asked in surprise.

"Yes, please," Lavina replied. "I have heard of your wonderful horses and I would like more than anything else to ride one of them."

"You are quite sure you can manage one?" the Marquis asked.

Lavina laughed.

"Quite...quite sure," she replied. "I have ridden since I could crawl, so please give me something spirited and a good jumper."

The Marquis stared at her.

"Now you are really surprising me," he said, "and are you telling me that your friends also ride?"

"Like ducks can swim," Lavina laughed, "and they have all brought their habits and will be very disappointed if you shut up your horses and say they are too good for us."

"I would never say that," the Marquis assured her. "At the same time, Vina, I did not anticipate that was what you would want."

"Talk to Kitty, and she will tell you better than I can that is what we are longing to do."

"Then, of course, it is what you *shall* do," the Marquis said, "and are you suggesting you will be down for breakfast?"

"But of course!"

She thought he was surprised, and that he looked at her questioningly.

He had never entertained anybody from the Theatrical World who, when they had the chance, did not lie in bed until nearly midday.

"What time do you usually have breakfast?" Lavina asked.

"To-morrow it will be from about eight-thirty onwards," the Marquis replied, "but I doubt if anyone will be down until after nine."

Lavina thought this was very late, but she did not say so.

They reached the bottom of the stairs, and she held out her hand.

"Thank you very, very much for a wonderful evening!" she said. "And thank you more than I can say for showing me your precious treasure from Tibet."

She drew in a deep breath before she added:

"I shall go to sleep thinking of it and perhaps I shall dream of where it comes from so that you will know where to send it back."

"Why are you so certain that I am willing to part

89

with it?" the Marquis asked. "It cost me a lot of money, and, like you, I find it very interesting and different from anything else I own."

"It can...never really...be yours," Lavina said quietly.

As the Marquis looked at her in astonishment she walked up the stairs.

He watched her until she reached the top.

She did not look back as he expected.

He had never met a woman who had left him without a backward glance.

Without smiling at him invitingly and, where a Gaiety Girl was concerned, that was definitely the right word.

As Lavina disappeared, he walked back to the Drawing-Room.

He was finding it difficult to ignore what she had said to him.

chapter five

LAVINA came down to breakfast punctually at eight-thirty.

She found to her surprise that the only other person there was the Marquis.

He rose from the table as she entered and said:

"Good-morning! You are more punctual than I believed possible!"

"I am usually downstairs before this," Lavina answered without thinking.

She saw the silver entrée dishes on the side-table and walked towards it.

She remembered her mother telling her that in big houses the servants did not wait at breakfast.

"It is difficult to know what to choose to eat from this enormous display!" she said.

"Are you hungry?" the Marquis asked.

He was thinking as he spoke that most of the

Gaiety Girls with whom he had been involved were very careful what they ate.

George Edwardes was insistent on their waists not being more than eighteen inches.

Most of them would therefore only pick at the delicious food that was served at Romano's.

He was also certain that when it came to their own meals they ate frugally, not to save money, because there was always plenty of that, but to preserve their figures.

"When I look at these dishes," Lavina replied, "I know I am going to eat a very large breakfast."

She helped herself to food from three different dishes as she spoke.

Then she came to the table smiling.

They were joined a few minutes later by Rupert and two other men.

But it was after nine o'clock before any of the other girls appeared.

"You went to bed early!" Katherine said in a slightly accusing voice. "We went much later, which this morning I know was a mistake!"

The Marquis laughed.

"You are usually much later because the Theatre does not end until eleven o'clock and then you go on to supper with one of your admirers."

Katherine knew she had made a mistake, and she answered quickly:

"But I do not have the chance of riding anything so spectacular as one of your horses, so I am quite content to stay in bed in the morning."

Lavina thought she had retrieved what was a gaffe very cleverly.

But she was glad she had not made it herself.

The others joined them one by one and it was nearly half-past-nine before breakfast was finished.

The Marquis announced that the horses were waiting for them outside.

Katherine hurried down the steps with Lavina following her.

She realised when they reached the horses why Katherine was in such a hurry.

"This is the horse I want to ride!" she said, patting a large stallion who had, Lavina thought, Arab blood in him.

Realising that Katherine had chosen, she herself took a chestnut which a groom was finding it hard to hold.

The Marquis had waited politely for the other Girls to leave the Breakfast-Room.

By the time he came outside Katherine and Lavina were in the saddle.

He walked quickly to where Lavina was controlling her obstreperous mount.

"That horse will be too much for you!" he said sharply. "I intended to let Rupert ride him."

Lavina smiled.

"It is too late," she said, "I have staked my claim! I shall be very upset if you give Rufus to somebody else!"

She had been told the horse's name by the groom.

As she spoke she bent forward to pat the chestnut's neck.

She talked to him in the soft, soothing voice her father had taught her to use.

The Marquis watched her.

Then, as if he felt it would be uncomfortable to make a fuss, he mounted his own stallion.

The other girls were helped into the saddle before the men mounted the horses that were left.

As they rode off, Lavina realised that Katherine had deliberately chosen those among her friends who were really good riders.

She was making every effort to impress the Marquis.

As she pushed her own horse ahead, she looked like a very beautiful Amazon going into battle.

The Marquis led the way to flat ground on which at the far end was his private race-course.

First, however, they rode for nearly half-a-mile, which took some of the freshness out of Rufus.

He was one of the most superb horses Lavina had ever ridden.

The Earl of Kenwick's stable was very good.

But, as Rupert had told her, the Marquis's was the best in the whole country.

When they reached the race-course the Marquis said:

"I do not want to disappoint you Girls, but the jumps have been prepared for a Steeple-Chase I am giving the week after next. They are particularly high, as I am making the course as difficult as possible for my riders, who, needless to say, are all men!"

Lavina could see the jumps were unusual.

"However," the Marquis went on, "there are some good hedges a little farther on. I suggest you follow me and I will show you where you can jump."

While he was talking, Lavina was aware that Katherine was eyeing the fences on the race-course.

As the Marquis was about to move on, she touched her horse with her whip and swept towards the first fence.

There was an exclamation from several of the men.

The Marquis pulled in his horse and watched her with a grim expression on his face.

Then, as she reached the jump, she swept over it with the ease of the exceptionally fine rider she was.

"Bravo!" the man called George exclaimed, who had sat next to her last night at dinner.

Lavina had learnt that he was the Earl of Morne, son of the Marquis of Mornecliff.

"She was fortunate," the Marquis said, and two or three others echoed his words. "Come along, the rest of you! I do not want any of my guests to have a broken neck!"

It was then, as she was about to follow him, that Lavina thought he was being very dictatorial.

Any good rider should be allowed to choose for him or herself what they were capable if doing.

She therefore touched Rufus very lightly with her whip and he responded immediately.

She had almost reached the jump before the Marquis realised what she was doing.

"Stop, Vina!" he shouted. "Stop at once!"

He was too late.

Rufus jumped the fence, not as well as Katherine's horse had done, Lavina thought, but still with three or four inches to spare.

He made a perfect landing on the other side.

Lavina realised as he did so that, in front of her, Katherine was taking the next fence.

She was just about to follow her when the Marquis came over the fence she had just jumped in magnificent style.

He landed, and his horse drew up alongside Rufus.

"You are not to follow Katie!" he said sharply.

"Why . . . not?"

Lavina was feeling a little breathless from the jump.

She had arranged her riding-hat firmly on her head.

She had pinned her hair so neatly that she looked as if she had done nothing more than a gentle trot.

"Because I say so," the Marquis replied. "I told you these jumps were very high. You nearly gave me a heart-attack just now. I thought it impossible for you to land without a bad fall."

"I consider that a little insulting!" Lavina replied. "I told you that I had ridden ever since I could crawl, and these fences would be too high only if I were riding an inferior animal!"

She smiled at the Marquis as she spoke and he said firmly:

"As your host and the owner of the horse you are riding, you will please do as I say!"

Her eyes met his as he spoke, and she felt that for the moment they crossed swords.

Then, because she had no wish to quarrel with him, she surrendered.

"Very well, My Lord, I will obey you, but reluctantly!"

"So I should hope," the Marquis said, "and perhaps I should reward you with something which you will enjoy more than risking your neck."

Lavina did not answer.

She did not wish to say that she would accept a present like Millicent, then disappear so that it would be impossible for her to receive it.

She just rode on, only bending forward to pat Rufus, who, whatever the Marquis might say, would have carried her safely over the other fences.

They rode until luncheontime, then turned back towards the house.

All the girls were receiving fulsome compliments from the men for the way they rode.

"I had no idea that Gaiety Girls could do anything more arduous than dance!" one of them said.

"Then I hope you have changed your opinion," Elizabeth replied, "and in future appreciate us a great deal more than you have in the past!"

"I think that would be impossible!" the man riding beside her said. "And you know as well as I do that you are all so incredibly beautiful that you need do nothing else but just allow us to look at you."

"I have a great many other things I want to do," Elizabeth answered.

The man to whom she was speaking moved his horse a little nearer to hers.

"I will tell you what I want when we are alone," he said.

There was a deep note in his voice that had not been there before.

Lavina, who was just behind them, realised that Elizabeth looked at him provocatively before she said:

"I think that might be difficult, as I am sure our

host has a very exciting programme for us this evening."

As they moved on, the man was obviously expostulating with Elizabeth.

Lavina thought with amusement that she, like all the other girls, was being very clever.

They were attracting the men as Katherine had intended.

At the same time, they were making it difficult for anyone to become intimate with them.

It had crossed her mind, when she agreed to Katherine's suggestion, that the Gaiety Girls were actresses.

She knew that they were frowned upon by the more respectable people in Society.

And of course the mothers of *débutantes* would not allow their daughters to find themselves in a "difficult" situation.

She did not know exactly what that might be.

Except that the men in the house-party might try to be familiar, perhaps put an arm around them or attempt to kiss their lips.

She knew that was something that would frighten her.

She wanted to ask Katherine what she should do if that happened.

Yet she felt too shy.

She finally decided that the one thing to avoid was to find herself alone with any of the Marquis's friends.

It had never crossed her mind, when the Marquis had shown her his treasures, that he was a man and she was alone with him.

Now she told herself she could certainly not find fault with anything he had said or done.

She supposed, despite everything that had been said about his obsession for Gaiety Girls, that she, at any rate, did not attract him.

As they rode back to the house she was thinking how brilliantly he rode.

It was as if he were a part of his horse.

It was then she wondered if the Gaiety Girls with whom he spent his time allowed him to kiss them after he had taken them out to supper.

Perhaps they fell in love with him.

'He is rather frightening,' she thought to herself. 'Yet he is very handsome and, as I thought when I first arrived, he has a personality which it would be impossible to ignore.'

'How could Katherine possibly have described him as "tiresome, conceited and stuck-up"? He was giving a wrong—entirely wrong—picture of himself to the world.'

Almost as if her thoughts made him aware of her, the Marquis pulled in his horse so that she came alongside him.

"You are looking very serious, Vina!" he said. "What are you thinking about?"

Without considering it, Lavina replied:

"I was thinking about you."

"I am flattered!" the Marquis said. "And what were you thinking?"

He thought he knew all the answers to that question.

But Lavina thought for a moment before she answered:

"I was thinking...you had a very strong...vibrant...personality and yet you are giving a wrong impression of yourself to the world!"

The Marquis looked at her in sheer astonishment.

"What do you mean by that?"

Because she realised she had said something which was faintly rude, Lavina said quickly:

"I...I am sorry...I just said what was in my mind...and it is something I...should not have done."

"On the contrary, I am interested," the Marquis said, "but I realise we have no time to talk about it now."

He had said that because they were back at the court-yard in front of the house.

The grooms were waiting to take their horses.

Lavina drew Rufus to a standstill.

When she would have slipped down from the saddle, the Marquis was beside her and lifted her to the ground.

Because she was so light, he seemed to hold her a little longer than was necessary before he put her down.

She was very conscious of his nearness and of his strength.

She was also aware of the strange feeling in her heart which she had felt before.

"I do not have to tell you how well you ride," the Marquis said.

As he spoke, he still had his hands on her waist.

She felt it was difficult to move away from him.

Her eyes closed slightly before his, and there was a flush on her cheeks as she replied:

"Thank . . . you."

Then, because she felt shy, she hurried into the house and up the stairs to change.

When she reached her room, she found to her surprise that the Housekeeper was there.

"Good-morning!" she said.

"Good-morning, Miss! You'll find all your clothes in th' Queen's Room which is where you'll be sleeping to-night."

She spoke in a somewhat sharp voice and Lavina asked in surprise:

"Why have I been moved?"

There was a moment's pause before the Housekeeper answered:

"Your fire's smoking an' His Lordship said th' room was to be closed 'til th' Sweep's been."

"Oh, I understand," Lavina said, "but what a nuisance it must be for you. Perhaps there's an old bird's nest blocking the chimney, as happened once at home."

The Housekeeper, however, did not seem to wish to chat.

She merely escorted Lavina to the other end of the corridor.

They walked quite a long way.

It occurred to Lavina that it was strange there should be no room nearer to the one where she had been sleeping.

She found, however, that the room into which the Housekeeper showed her was even more impressive than the one she had left.

The huge canopied bed had carved gilt posts and was hung with exquisite needlework curtains.

The pictures were very fine and so was the furniture.

She was sure that it was one of the main State-Rooms.

The Housekeeper did not wait for her to ask any questions.

She left, and the maid who had unpacked her trunk came hurrying in to help her change.

"This is a very beautiful room!" Lavina remarked.

"That's wot I always thinks, Miss," the maid replied. "But yer should see 'is Lordship's."

"I imagine that is even more impressive," Lavina said.

"It is, an' the bed could 'old five people easy, Miss, an' the coronet on top o' it's as large as a football!"

Lavina laughed.

She thought it was a room she would like to see.

But she knew that was something she could not ask the Marquis.

She was, however, very content with the room in which she was now.

The dressing-table had an oval mirror with a frame carved with cupids and a valance made of Valentian lace.

The windows had a different view from the rooms she had just left.

Now she could see a rose-garden, smooth green lawns, and beyond them what she thought was a Maze.

'I shall never have time to see it all,' she thought with a little sigh.

The maid helped her into the elaborate gown

which Katherine had chosen for her to wear in the afternoon.

It was blue, and Lavina would not have thought of wearing any jewellery if the maid had not suggested it.

"Wear yer pearl necklace, Miss. It'll look ever so lovely round yer neck."

It seemed over-dressed for the daytime, but Lavina did as the maid suggested.

She also remembered just at the last minute to touch up her make-up.

After her ride her lips were almost their natural colour and she needed a little extra mascara on her eye-lashes.

When she hurried to the top of the stairs Katherine was just coming from her room.

She looked at her critically before she said in a low voice:

"You look fine, Lavina. It was clever of you to remember your make-up. I have just prevented Suzana from going down without any!"

As she spoke, Suzana came running up to them.

"I am sorry, Katherine!" she said. "It was very silly of me, but I was hurrying because Rupert said he had something to tell me."

As she finished speaking she ran down the stairs ahead.

Katherine looked after her with a worried expression on her face.

"I wonder if there is anything wrong?" she said.

"No, of course not," Lavina replied. "If there was, Rupert would tell you first."

"I hope you are right," Katherine muttered.

They reached the hall and were shown not into the Study but into another room which Lavina had not seen before.

It was just as magnificent as the others. Only it had more pictures, and most of them were by French artists.

Lavina had always longed to see a real Fragonard or a Boucher.

She was moving from one wall to the next when the Marquis joined her.

"I thought you would enjoy this room," he said.

"It is simply wonderful!" Lavina exclaimed.

She had not taken her eyes off the pictures as she spoke.

There was a twinkle in the Marquis's eyes.

When he was there it was not often that a woman looked at anything other than him.

Luncheon proved to be a delightful meal with everybody talking and laughing.

Each of them seemed to have a different point of view on every subject under discussion.

Lavina was aware that it was Katherine who had started controversy in the first place and kept the conversation going.

She thought how clever she was.

What was more, she was just the sort of wife the Marquis ought to have.

It was with difficulty that she prevented herself from suggesting such an idea to him.

After luncheon there had been some talk of going riding, but it had started to rain.

The Marquis, therefore, took them to a room in

one of the Wings, where there was every sort of game.

There was a Billiard and a Ping-Pong table.

There was Backgammon, Darts, Chess, and every other amusing game including Games of Chance which had come from France.

Everything seemed to make them laugh so that Lavina thought it would be impossible to enjoy herself more.

The hours seemed to slip by until it was time to rest before dinner.

Lavina had a bath in front of the fire and put on her other evening gown.

That too was blue and embroidered all over with tiny diamanté which glistened as she moved.

Diamantés shimmered on the flounces at the back, and round her neck.

She was just wondering whether she should wear the diamond and torquoise necklace for the second time when there was a knock at the door.

Just as had happened last evening, flowers were presented to her on a tray.

"I had forgotten about them!" Lavina exclaimed. "What shall we choose?"

The maid inspected the tray which was carried by a footman very carefully.

"There's some little lilies, Miss," she said, "an' they somehow seems right for yer."

"Then of course I will wear them." Lavina smiled.

The maid took some for her hair.

Then Lavina noticed there were a few more made into a neat little bunch, as if for a Gentleman's lapel.

"Do you think I could have those too?" she asked

the maid. "I could wear them at my throat."

"That's a good idea, Miss," the maid agreed.

She fixed the posey to a piece of velvet ribbon.

It was certainly very becoming, and although Lavina did not realise it, made her look younger than ever.

She went downstairs.

As one of the men said, "She looked as if she had stepped out of a rain-cloud," she was aware that the Marquis was at her side.

"To-night we have drawn for partners at dinner," he said, "and I have drawn you."

She gave him a little smile and he said:

"I hope you are pleased."

"Of course I am!"

They went into dinner.

It seemed to Lavina that every man had drawn the girl to whom he had been paying attention all day.

Then she saw there was a present on each of their plates.

For Lavina there was a pretty little box.

When she opened it she found it contained a powder-puff and some powder.

A tiny mirror was inserted into the lid.

"Thank you, thank you very much!" she said to the Marquis. "It is the prettiest present I have ever had!"

"I expect you to be saying that to me many times in the future," he replied.

She did not understand for a moment what he meant.

When she did she blushed and looked away.

Unexpectedly the Marquis asked sharply:

"Who gave you the necklace you were wearing last night?"

Because she could not think of an answer, Lavina pretended she had not heard the question.

She bent sideways to look at the present which Doris had been given.

She hoped the Marquis would not ask her again about her necklace.

After dinner there was an Orchestra.

To her surprise, Lavina found herself dancing with the Marquis more than with anybody else.

Then Rupert asked her to dance.

As they swung round the floor he said in a low voice:

"Kathy has decided that, as some of the men are returning to London to-morrow, you will all have to leave very early before anyone is aware of it! She is arranging for you to be called at a quarter-to-six. I will see that the carriages are round at half-past."

"I will be ready," Lavina said.

She realised as she spoke that Katherine was right.

It would be a great mistake for the gentlemen who had been paying attention to the girls to be with them when they arrived in London.

They would certainly think it strange that they should all be going to a smart house off Grosvenor Square.

Everything so far had been such a success that it would be a disaster now if anything went wrong.

There was a Cotillion at which the Marquis had provided pretty prizes for the Ladies, and some ridiculous jokes for the men.

At last when it was nearly one o'clock they all began to drift upstairs to bed.

Lavina was beginning to feel tired because the ride in the morning had bean quite strenuous.

Also she had lain awake the night before worrying in case she should do something wrong.

The maid who had helped her undress left, yawning because she had waited up.

Lavina locked her door as Katherine had warned her she should do.

Having said her prayers, she got into bed.

The Marquis had installed electric light in most of the house.

But she had learnt that the State-Rooms like the one she was in had not been spoilt by anything so modern.

The only light therefore came from a small silver-gilt candelabrum by her bed.

Three gold cupids held up three candles.

Before she blew them out she had one more look at the lovely room.

As she did so, the mirror on the other side of the mantelpiece swung open.

It was then she realised it was attached to a door and not, as she had thought, to the wall.

As she stared in amazement the Marquis came into the room.

He was wearing a long robe with a frogged front which looked very military.

For the moment she did not realise that beneath it he was undressed.

"What...what has...happened? What is...
wrong?" she asked.

"There is nothing wrong," the Marquis replied as
he came towards her, "except that I have not said
good-night to you."

"Oh...but you did...at the bottom of...the
stairs," Lavina replied, "and I...thanked you for
the...wonderful evening!"

"It was not possible to say good-night properly
with so many people around us," the Marquis said.

He reached the bed and sat down on the side of it
facing her.

It was then Lavina said:

"I...I am sorry...but it is...wrong for you to be
here...and you must...go away at once...I...I
locked my...door."

"As you did last night,"

"H-how did you...know that?"

"My friends told me that to their surprise all the
Girls had locked their doors, and I did not think that
you would be the exception."

"No, of course...not," Lavina said, "but...I did
not realise there was...another door in this...
room."

The Marquis did not reply, and after a moment
she said:

"Please...go away...you know you...should
not...be here...talking to me and...my mother
would be...shocked."

"I understood your mother was dead."

"She is...but my father is alive...and he would
be...extremely angry!"

"As neither of them are with us," the Marquis said

with a slightly mocking note in his voice, "I do not think we need worry about them, and I want to tell you, Vina, how beautiful you are and how you attract me."

He reached out as he spoke and took her hand in both of his.

Because he was touching her, Lavina felt again that strange sensation in her breast.

There was a breathlessness which seemed to rise up through her throat.

"I have a lot to say to you," the Marquis said, "and I want to help you."

"Why . . . must we . . . talk about it . . . now?" Lavina asked.

"Because you are leaving to-morrow morning and I want you to know what I have been planning."

His fingers tightened on her hand, and she thought he came a little nearer to her.

"First," the Marquis said, "I intend to speak to George Edwardes to ensure that you are given an important part in *The Girl*, if that is what you want. Then I cannot allow you to go to Manchester or wherever it is you are playing next, and therefore I suggest you stay with me until the Show comes to London."

He smiled at her before he went on:

"I will find you an attractive house in Chelsea or St. John's Wood, whichever you prefer."

Lavina stared at him.

She did not understand what he was saying.

It was difficult to concentrate because she was so acutely aware that he was touching her.

His face, too, was very near to hers.

"I promise you I will make you very, very happy," the Marquis said. "You shall have the most beautiful gowns that London can provide and of course the jewellery to go with it."

"I...I do not know...what you are...saying to me," Lavina cried. "P-please...go...away!"

She tried to speak sharply and in a way to which the Marquis would listen.

Instead, her voice was very small and breathless.

"Now you are being unkind to me," the Marquis said.

He bent forward as he spoke and would have kissed her.

But before his lips could reach hers, she turned her head away.

He had released her hand and she was pushing him with all her strength to prevent him from coming any closer.

"You are so beautiful!" the Marquis said, putting his arms around her, "and I will teach you about love."

It was then Lavina gave a scream that was like that of a small animal caught in a trap.

Twisting from side to side, she cried:

"Go away...leave me...alone!"

It was something he had not expected, and the Marquis raised himself to look at her in surprise.

"What are you saying?" he asked. "What is upsetting you?"

"What you are...suggesting is...wrong and...wicked," Lavina said, "and you are...frightening me...please...please...go away. I am frightened."

The Marquis looked at her in sheer astonishment.

Then, as he saw the tears in her eyes and realised that she was in fact terrified, he asked:

"How can you be frightened? How can you talk to me like this unless you have a revulsion for me? Is that true?"

There was an incredulous note in his voice.

No woman had ever been repulsed by him.

"You are ... not to ... touch me," Lavina sobbed, "and ... of course I ... cannot do the ... evil thing you are ... asking me ... to do!"

"Evil?" the Marquis exclaimed.

Sitting up, he asked sharply:

"Now, answer me truthfully—who gave you the necklace you wore last night and the pearls you wore to-day?"

Lavina was just about to say it was Katherine, then, stumbling over her words, she said:

"I ... b-borrowed them ... from one of the ... g-girls."

"Is that true?" the Marquis asked. "Do you swear to me on everything you hold sacred that it is true?"

"It is ... true!"

The Marquis put out his hand and lifted her chin to turn her face up to his.

"Tell me something else," he said, "and again, it must be the truth."

He looked at her penetratingly.

Because she was wearing no mascara or other make-up on her face, he thought she looked very young and defenceless.

At the same time, she was, without exception, the loveliest woman he had ever seen.

"Tell me," he said, "and if you lie I shall know you

are lying. Has any man ever possessed you?"

For a moment Lavina did not understand what he was saying.

Then, as she looked up at him, he saw how shocked she was at the idea.

"How can you...think," she whispered, "I would do...anything that...would be a...sin against... God?"

The Marquis released her and stood up.

"I do not understand what is happening," he said, "but we will talk about it to-morrow, when you are not so upset."

The tears were running down her cheeks.

But she still managed to look at him through them while her lips were trembling.

chapter six

LAVINA awoke with a start and thought somebody was calling her.

It was dark outside, but the feeling she was wanted was insistent.

She thought she must be dreaming and settled down again against her pillows.

But the call was still there, so strong, that she realised what it was.

She could see, like a picture in front of her eyes in the darkness, the Emerald Buddha.

It seemed to be vibrating towards her, calling her, telling her something of importance.

She tried to concentrate.

Then she understood—the Emerald Buddha was calling the Marquis and it was important.

It was almost as if it spoke with a clear voice, telling her that the Marquis was wanted.

Lavina lit two candles.

Without even thinking it strange, she got out of bed.

She picked up her dressing-gown which the maid had left over a chair.

It was very different from what a Gaiety Girl would have worn.

It was just a simple garment she had made herself from some woollen material.

She put it on and buttoned it down the front.

It had a small collar edged with a frill of lace round her neck.

Then, without remembering her shoes, she pulled open the door which had the mirror on it.

She saw there was a Sitting-Room which she had not realised was there.

By the light of the candles behind her she found her way across the room.

She opened the door and found herself in a small lobby with two doors in it.

One led out into the corridor, the other into the Marquis's bed-room.

Lavina paused, thinking she must be absolutely certain the Marquis was wanted and she was not dreaming as she had thought at first.

Then, almost as if she were being ordered by a Power greater than herself, she opened the Marquis's door and went inside.

She expected the room to be in darkness; instead, he had pulled back the curtains.

The moonlight was streaming in. The sky was brilliant with stars.

She could see quite clearly the huge canopied bed

which the maid had described to her.

As she went up to it she could see the Marquis lying against his pillows fast asleep.

"Wake up, My Lord!" she said.

She spoke so quietly that it did not disturb him.

Putting out her hand, she touched his shoulder gently and instantly he was awake.

"What is it?" he asked.

Then he saw Lavina and exclaimed in sheer astonishment:

"Vina!"

"You are wanted," she said softly, "by the Emerald Buddha."

He stared at her.

"What are you talking about?"

"There is ... something happening ... downstairs," Lavina said, "and you are needed."

The Marquis thought that what he was hearing could not be true.

Without waiting for his answer, Lavina said:

"Please, come, I will wait ... outside the ... door."

She walked away from the bed as she spoke.

She found her way to the door which led into the corridor, and opened it.

Most of the lights had been extinguished, but there were just enough left for her to see quite clearly.

A minute later the Marquis joined her, wearing the long, frogged robe he had worn when he came into her room.

Vina did not speak, she merely looked up at him.

As if he thought it was impossible to go on questioning her, he merely said:

"We will go down by a side staircase."

She was aware he wanted this because there would be a footman on duty in the hall.

It would be a mistake for them to be seen together.

Without thinking, merely because she knew it was so important for him to go to the Buddha, she slipped her hand into his.

His fingers closed over hers.

He drew her towards the staircase which was only a short distance from his room.

It was wide enough for them to go down it hand-in-hand.

Again there was enough light left for them to see their way.

When they reached the Ground Floor the Marquis turned towards his Study.

It took them only a few seconds to reach the door.

He opened it—the light was on.

Then as they walked into the room the Marquis stood still in sheer astonishment.

The Emerald Buddha had been taken from the cabinet in which he had placed it.

Now it was standing on a table.

Kneeling in front of it were two men with their hands clasped together in prayer.

Before the Marquis could speak, one of the men rose from his knees.

Lavina saw that he was tall with white hair.

He was wearing some strange-looking monk's robes and a fur-trimmed hat.

She was sure they were the clothes worn by Tibetans.

The man turned towards the Marquis and, bowing to him, said in excellent English:

"I sent a message for you, Honourable Lord, so that I could tell you that I have brought you the greeting and blessing of the Abbot of the Gyagtse Monastery. He is deeply grateful that our most priceless treasure fell into your hands rather than into those who might have damaged or defaced it."

"How did you know it was I who had it?" the Marquis asked.

"It was stolen from us," the Tibetan replied, "by a Monk who was dismissed from our Monastery because he carried evil in his heart.

"The Lord Buddha had been covered during the Anniversary celebrations of the death of our Founder, and it was therefore some time before we learned of the loss, and by that time the thief had reached India."

"Where he approached me!" the Marquis replied.

"Exactly! But as I have said, it is very fortunate for us that you, Honourable Lord, were the purchaser."

"I still cannot understand how you learned this," the Marquis said, "and how you have been able to follow me here to my home."

The Tibetan smiled, and Lavina was sure he was a Lama of very high rank.

"We have our ways of knowing such things," he said quietly, "and now, having completed this long journey, I am asking you to give back to us what is the heart and inspiration of the two thousand Monks who dwell under our Holy roof."

The Lama paused and looked at the Buddha before he said:

"I need not tell you, Honourable Lord, what benefits will come from your generosity, and I have brought with me the money you gave the thief."

He drew a small bag from his robes as he spoke and held it out to the Marquis.

The Marquis did not take it, but said:

"I realise that I should be grateful for having possessed, if only for a short time, anything so Holy and so valuable to you. Keep the money and spend it on the travellers who seek your assistance or those who are too poor to help themselves."

The Lama's eyes seemed to light up.

"The Lord Buddha will bless you," he said, "and I promise, Honourable Lord, you will always be remembered in our prayers."

The bag of money disappeared into his robe, and he would have moved towards the table.

But the Marquis said:

"May I offer you some refreshment, and would you like to rest until morning?"

"Thank you," the Lama replied, "but we must hurry back from where we have come."

It was then that Lavina spoke for the first time:

"Would you...Reverend Lama...bless us...before you...go?"

"You are already blessed, my child," the Lama replied. "But I will give to you the special blessing of our Lord and Master."

Lavina went down on her knees.

As she did so, the Lama looked at the Marquis.

For a second he hesitated. Then he too knelt.

The Lama raised his hand and in a deep resonant voice which seemed to echo and re-echo round the room he blessed them.

Lavina did not understand the words, but there was no need for her to do so.

She could feel his faith that was indestructible vibrating all around her.

She looked up at him, and as she did so there was a blinding light, brilliant and dazzling, that enveloped her and the Marquis.

She shut her eyes because it was impossible to keep them open.

Then, as the Lama's voice died away, there was silence, although the light was still there.

* * *

The Marquis opened his eyes feeling that what he had just experienced could not be true.

Then he saw that the Emerald Buddha had gone and so had the Lama and his assistant.

For a moment he felt that they had never been there at all and he had only been dreaming.

The Study was just as it always was except that there was a cold draught from the windows.

He rose to his feet and, as he was about to shut it, he heard the sound of wheels and horses' hoofs in the distance.

He knew then that his strange guests had gone and were on their way back to Tibet.

He closed the window.

As he turned back he saw Lavina was still kneeling, her head thrown back as if she were still looking at the Buddha.

For a moment he just looked at her.

Then her eyes opened.

He was about to speak to her when he realised she

was still swept away by the ecstasy she had experienced when the Lama blessed them.

Without saying one word the Marquis picked her up in his arms.

He was aware as he did so that her feet were bare.

She made a little murmur and turned her face against his shoulder.

She was very light, and he carried her from the room along the corridor and up the stairs the way they had come.

He had left the door of his room ajar and he carried her through it and into the Sitting-Room.

The light from the open door guided him.

Only when he had carried Lavina into her own bed-room did he put her down gently on the floor.

It was then he spoke for the first time.

"Go to bed, my darling," he said, "we will talk about this to-morrow."

She looked up at him as she spoke and was so irresistibly lovely that he bent his head and his lips just touched hers.

It was a kiss without passion, a kiss almost of reverence.

Then, as he felt her quiver, he turned and walked away, shutting the door quietly behind him.

* * *

Lavina felt as if she had been asleep for only a few minutes before the maid knocked on the door.

She pulled back the curtains.

Lavina was aware, because she had locked her door last night, that the maid had come through the room she had passed through to find the Marquis.

It was then that the amazing things that had happened last night came back to her mind.

She felt as if the blessing the Lama had given her had enriched her so that she was no longer the person she had been.

Then the maid said:

"You'll 'ave to 'urry, Miss; the carriages'll be round at six-thirty!"

Lavina got out of bed and the maid started to pack her clothes into the trunk.

There were fortunately not many of them, and the trunk was ready when two footmen came to collect it.

When they had gone, Lavina put on her hat with the feathers.

She thought it strange to wear anything so smart as an ermine cape so early in the morning.

She was ready before the hands on the clock said half-past.

She collected her hand-bag, taking from it the tip for the maid who had looked after her.

"Thank yer very much, Miss!" the maid said. "An' I 'opes some day t'come t'London and see yer on th' stage, if I sits up in th' Gallery!"

"I hope you will be able to do that," Lavina replied, "and thank you very much for all you have done for me."

"It's bin a real pleasure, Miss," the maid replied.

Lavina hurried from her room and down the stairs.

She was not surprised to find Katherine and nearly all the other girls assembled in the hall.

They were standing in silence.

She knew that it was on Katherine's orders that they did not speak.

As she reached the others, Rupert, who was standing at the front-door, beckoned to them.

They hurried down the steps and into the carriages which were waiting.

Lavina found herself in the first one with Katherine, Millicent, and Rupert.

It was the way they had arrived at Sherwood Park.

The horses moved off and, as they passed over the bridge that spanned the lake, Rupert said to his sister:

"Millicent has something to tell you."

Katherine looked surprised at the way he spoke and asked:

"What is it, Millicent?"

Millicent drew in her breath before she said:

"I have promised to marry George and, oh, Katherine, I am so happy!"

"George?" Katherine questioned. "Do you mean the Earl of Morne?"

Millicent nodded.

"He asked me to marry him last night and, dearest, do not be angry with me, but I had to tell him the truth!"

Katherine gave an exclamation and Rupert said quickly:

"George came to my room and told me what had happened. He said he is madly in love with Millicent and was prepared to marry her even if she had been a Gaiety Girl. The fact that she is not makes it of course very much easier, and his parents will be delighted. So, I am sure, will the Duke."

Millicent gave a little laugh.

"Even Papa, fussy though he is, could not object to George!"

"No, of course not," Katherine said. "I am sure you will be very happy."

"I know I will," Millicent said firmly.

"What George had asked, however," Rupert interposed, "is that in the circumstances we should never tell anyone, including the Marquis, who you really are."

There was a little silence before Katherine said somewhat reluctantly:

"I suppose I must... agree to... that."

"Of course you must," her brother said, "and George is being very careful about it. He says that he will be obliged, as the Marquis is one of his greatest friends, to invite him to the wedding, but he is going to try to keep him from meeting Millicent for as long as possible."

"You do not think he will recognise her?" Katherine asked.

"Not if they do not marry for a month or so," Rupert replied, "and you know as well as I do that people see what they expect to see."

Katherine laughed.

"That is true."

"What George is nervous about is that if the Marquis should see Millicent with you, Lavina, or any of the others, he might realise there is a strange resemblance to the Gaiety Girls he entertained, simply because there are two or three who remind him of Dolly, Betty, Kathy, and Vina!"

They laughed because of the way Rupert said the

names, making them sound so silly.

"I suppose you are right," Katherine said. "I can hardly bear to think we went to all that trouble for nothing!"

"What you have proved," Rupert said, "is that Gaiety Girls can have brains as well as beauty. You will have to leave the Marquis to be convinced by somebody else that *débutantes* are not all 'nincompoops.'"

They drove on.

Now Lavina was thinking not of Millicent, but of what happened last night.

She was remembering how understanding and generous the Marquis had been to the Lama, how without protesting he had allowed him to take back the Emerald Buddha.

Then she knew without even remembering the touch of his lips on hers that she loved him.

She had loved him, she thought, ever since they had talked the first night at dinner.

Although she had been horrified at what he had suggested, he had in fact left her.

That he had not insisted on staying made her realise now how wonderful he was.

He might have forced himself on her and kissed her as he had wanted to do.

He might have touched her and frightened her even more than she had been at the time.

"He is everything a man should be!" she told herself.

Then she wanted to cry because she would never see him again.

Even before Katherine said it, she knew she would

now have to return to the country.

They arrived in London and were driven to the house off Grosvenor Square, where they would change.

It was there that Katherine said the words she was expecting.

"You know, dearest," she said, "that I had wanted you to stay with me in London and take you to Balls and parties as I promised, but . . ."

"It is all right," Lavina interrupted. "I know I have to disappear, and of course I should go back to look after Papa."

"I shall bring you to London next Spring," Katherine promised determinedly, "and nothing shall stop me! But you do understand that for the moment we must think of Millicent and make sure the Duke and Duchess never have the slightest inkling of what she has been doing."

"I understand," Lavina said.

She went back with Katherine to Kenwick House to collect the few things she had left behind.

They had luncheon alone because Rupert had not yet returned.

Having accompanied them to the Halt, he had returned to Sherwood Park.

They had not travelled in the Marquis's private railway carriages because he had not expected them to go so early.

They had a First Class compartment to themselves and Rupert had provided them with breakfast in a hamper.

After luncheon, Katherine told Lavina there was a train at two-thirty which would take her home.

"You will be back before it is dark, dearest," she said, "and I am sending one of the housemaids with you, as I do not think you should travel alone."

Lavina did not protest that this was unnecessary.

She was glad to think that somebody would be there to look after her.

She thought too that she would not be nervous as she had been on the journey to London.

She saw another trunk standing beside hers.

As it was being carried out to the carriage, she looked at it in surprise and Katherine said:

"It is just a few of my gowns which I thought you might find useful, and also the habit you wore at Sherwood Park. If you remove the braiding and narrow the shoulders a little, you will not feel embarrassed in it."

"You are so kind to me," Lavina said.

"I am trying to be," Katherine replied, "but Millicent has messed up all my plans. Now I shall see that they start again the very day after she has married her Earl and set off on her honeymoon!"

She kissed Lavina affectionately and said:

"Thank you for being so helpful. No one could have been more convincing in the part than you were, nor so clever with the Marquis!"

Lavina knew this was something she did not want to talk about.

She therefore said quickly:

"I had better go in case I miss the train."

She kissed Katherine again and drove off towards the station.

It was not a very long journey, nor a very tiring one.

Lavina felt, however, that she was leaving behind her something very precious.

It was something she would never find again.

She knew what it was, but she did not want to admit it, even to herself.

*   *   *

Lavina found, as she expected, that Nanny had looked after her father perfectly and he really had not missed her.

"I have nearly three chapters to read to you," he said triumphantly.

Then as an afterthought he asked:

"Have you had a good time?"

"It was lovely seeing Katherine again," Lavina replied.

She did not want him to ask too many questions, but she need not have worried.

He had reached a very important part in his book and found it difficult to talk about anything else.

Because it was about India, Lavina kept remembering how the Marquis had said he had been there, and how they had talked about it.

Only when she went to bed did she face the fact that this was the end.

She would never see the Marquis again.

It was then the love she felt for him seemed to sweep over her like a tidal wave.

It was so intense, so irresistible that she felt as if she could hear him calling her as she had heard the Emerald Buddha.

Then she told herself it was just her imagination.

To the Marquis she was just a Gaiety Girl and someone who could have no real significance in his life.

She could almost hear Rupert saying how many Gaiety Girls had "passed through his hands."

She was not certain what that meant.

She supposed that he had offered them what he had offered her: a house in Chelsea or St. John's Wood, beautiful gowns and jewels.

She wished she could have told him that she wanted none of those things.

She only wanted something he was not prepared to give anyone, and that was his heart.

"He would...not have...understood," she told herself miserably.

It was then the tears came, tears that seemed to rend her whole being apart.

She knew, like many other women before her, that she had fallen in love with a man who was as inaccessible as the moon.

He would never love her in the same way she loved him.

She knew, when they knelt together to receive the blessing of the Lama, it had joined them irrevocably.

They were no longer two people, but one.

The blessing of the Buddha had united their souls.

"I love him...I love him!" Lavina murmured over and over again.

As she cried she felt the Marquis was as far away from her as if he, like the Emerald Buddha, lived on an inaccessible mountain in Tibet.

*   *   *

The Marquis awoke rather later than usual.

After he had left Lavina last night, it had been a long time before he had fallen asleep.

He had lain awake thinking of the extraordinary appearance of the Lama and his assistant Monk.

It seemed impossible to believe that they had managed to trace him back to England.

Also they had entered his house without his being aware of it.

He had heard when he had been in India of sorcerers and sages.

Some of them could look into a bowl of water and see what they wished to see if they said the right prayers.

He supposed that was what had happened.

At the same time, it seemed extraordinary that having come to his house they should also know exactly where the Emerald Buddha was.

It was also strange that, while he had not heard them calling for him, Lavina had.

He remembered how she had felt the vibrations of the Buddha when he showed it to her.

She had said immediately that it was Holy and had prayed to it.

'She is a most extraordinary person!' he thought.

He admitted she attracted him more than any other woman had ever done.

There was so much he wanted to talk about, and he also wanted to be with her.

Because he exercised self-control, he had been able to leave her alone in her bed-room to go to his own.

He was still puzzled and bewildered by the way she had behaved when he had tried to make love to her.

Never in his many associations with women had any of them screamed or tried to fight themselves free of him.

No woman had ever thought what he had suggested to them was wrong, wicked, or, as Lavina had said, evil.

"How could I have guessed, how could I have imagined," he asked himself, "that being a Gaiety Girl she was so pure and untouched?"

He knew from the things she had said that she was also very innocent.

He had at first suspected it was an act.

Perhaps somebody had suggested to her it was a way to attract him.

But it was difficult to question her sincerity.

The more he had seen of her, the more he talked to her, the more bewildered he became.

How was it possible that she could be so beautiful and yet appear so completely ignorant of life, of men, and of the world in general?

He realised she was very young.

But he knew the Gaiety Girls in the Provinces were fêted, and men must have pursued her from the moment she appeared on the stage.

It therefore made it difficult for him to believe she was not play-acting rather than being herself.

"I do not understand her!" he said to himself as he tossed and turned.

Finally, dawn had broken before he fell asleep.

When he awoke he realised that his valet had come

to call him and he had not been aware of it.

Beside his bed was the inevitable pot of tea, and two wafer-thin slices of bread, and some butter.

He never ate them, but everybody in the house was always called in the same way.

So they were brought to his room every morning.

He glanced at the clock and realised it was after eight.

He thought it unlikely that Vina would come down early to breakfast after such a disturbed night.

Then he remembered that, unlike most Gaiety Girls he knew, she had said she was used to rising early.

Perhaps she would wish to ride before they all went back to London.

He remembered how well she had ridden and so, as it happened, had the other girls.

He had once allowed a Gaiety Girl to ride one of his horses in Rotten Row.

He had prevented her from doing so ever again.

She had been a very inexperienced rider who was what his groom called "ham-fisted" with the reins.

She was also, although she would not have acknowledged it, frightened of the horse, even though it was a particularly quiet one.

Vina, like her friend Kathy, had taken one of the highest fences on the race-course.

He had thought for one terrifying moment that she would break her neck.

That was the moment when he had realised how much she meant to him.

He could not believe his own feelings.

He had enjoyed the Gaiety Girls with whom he

had spent so much of his time.

But none of them had been indispensable.

When he grew bored with one, there was always another to take her place.

He was quite certain, however, there would never be anyone to take Vina's place.

She was unique.

When he was dressed he said to his valet:

"What time has it been arranged for the young ladies to be taken to the Halt?"

"They've already left, M'Lord!"

"What do you mean—left?" the Marquis asked sharply.

"They left at six-thirty, M'Lord."

The Marquis stiffened. Then he said angrily:

"Why did nobody tell me?"

"I thought Your Lordship must 'ave known," the valet answered.

The Marquis put on his riding-jacket and went downstairs.

There were several men in the Breakfast-Room, including Rupert Wick.

When the Marquis walked in, they bade him good-morning, but he did not answer.

He walked up to Rupert, who was sitting at the sideboard, helping himself from one of the dishes.

"Why did you not tell me the Girls were leaving so early?" he demanded.

"I thought you knew," Rupert replied vaguely. "They had to be in London early and I think they leave to-day to appear in *The Girl* in another City."

"Which City?" the Marquis asked.

"I cannot remember," Rupert replied after a moment's pause. "It might be Manchester, but I am really not sure."

The Marquis turned away to go to his place at the top of the table.

As he did so, Rupert's eyes met those of the Earl of Morne.

Both men looked slightly apprehensive.

chapter seven

Lavina wanted to go riding.

She hesitated over whether or not she should wear the habit Katherine had given her.

Then she asked herself: what did it matter what she looked like?

She would meet nobody on her ride, and her father would not notice if she had come down in sackcloth.

She walked round to the stables to find that the old groom who had been with them for years had her horse ready.

She had always been proud of Swallow.

But there was no use pretending he was anything like Rufus or any of the other horses belonging to the Marquis.

All she really wanted at the moment was to get away by herself and think.

She rode into the Park and, passing under the trees, made for the woods.

She had loved the woods ever since she was a child.

She had believed there were elves under the trees and nymphs in the pool that lay in the centre of it.

To-day the magic was gone.

All she could see was the Marquis's grey eyes, all she could hear was his voice.

She kept thinking of how he had carried her upstairs after they had been blessed by the Lama.

Even through the ecstasy to which the blessing had taken her she was conscious of the strength of his arms and his closeness.

As he had kissed her good-night she had felt as if the stars were twinkling in her breast.

The moonlight had streaked through her like lightning.

"I love . . . him! I love . . . him!"

The birds were singing these words as they flew into the sky at her approach.

There had been a hard frost during the night, and she took Swallow carefully in case the path was slippery.

The firs made her think it was Christmas and the elms and oaks had lost their leaves.

When she had been young she had thought that nothing was more beautiful than the skeleton of a leafless tree against the sky.

It moved her in a strange way.

It was almost the same as she had felt when she had looked at the Emerald Buddha.

She thought of the Lama carrying it back in triumph to the Monastery in Tibet.

She imagined the joy with which it would be received, the reverence with which the Monks would kneel in front of it to pray to the Lord Buddha.

She rode on, trying to tell herself she had enjoyed the strange and wonderful experience.

It was greedy to ask for more.

Yet her whole being was calling for Sherwood Park and the Marquis.

"I have to be sensible about this," she said beneath her breath as if she were speaking to a child. "He will go back to London and never think of me again. How can I be so foolish as to cry for the unobtainable?"

She emerged from the woods and rode Swallow over a flat piece of land on which she had often ridden with Katherine and Rupert.

It seemed desolate and barren without them.

She remembered how they had laughed when they had been at dinner in the Marquis's house.

"Perhaps when I go to London I shall meet somebody like him," she told herself.

Then she knew that there could not be another man exactly like him, nor another man who would capture her heart.

She remembered her mother, saying:

"When I met your father I knew there was no other man in the world except him, and he felt the same about me."

'I feel the same,' Lavina thought, 'and that means I shall be an Old Maid.'

She wondered what she would do when her father was no longer there.

She thought perhaps she could teach in a School

or look after young children.

It shot through her mind that what she would like more than anything in the world would be a child of her own, a son who would grow up to be like the Marquis.

She wondered why he had ever got the reputation of being conceited and stuck up.

She could remember all too vividly how generous and understanding he had been to the Lama.

No man, whoever he was, could have behaved more perfectly.

"I love . . . him!"

The same words were back on her lips.

As she turned for home she thought the world was dark and cold.

There was nothing to look forward to.

She had been back for four days when Nanny said:

"I don't know what's the matter with you. You looks so peaky. I only hopes you're not sickening for anything."

Lavina could have told her she was suffering from love.

She cried into her pillow every night.

Only by a superhuman effort did she manage to talk normally and smile occasionally during the day.

"What you want is a companion of your own age!" Nanny went on. "When is Lady Katherine coming home?"

"I have no idea, Nanny," Lavina replied. "She is having a wonderful time in London, but I expect they will be back before Christmas, and of course the Earl will have his shooting parties at the end of November."

"Well, His Lordship won' invite you!" Nanny said tartly. "But I 'spect Her Ladyship'll be having some friends to stay!"

"I am sure she will," Lavina agreed.

She thought the one person who would not be present would be the Marquis.

Now she wondered if Katherine would be able to avoid seeing him in London.

She supposed that would be easy if he continued to spend his time with the Gaiety Girls.

When she reached home, the old groom took Swallow into his stall and started to rub him down.

Lavina went into the house and up to her bedroom to change.

It was really unnecessary because she would change again for dinner with her father.

It was her mother who had always been insistent that when she came in from riding she should take off her habit and her boots and put on a gown.

She was deep in her thoughts.

Only when she looked in the mirror to tidy her hair did she realise that she had put on a pretty afternoon gown that was blue.

It was the same blue as the gown she had worn at Sherwood Park.

She had not been thinking when she took it out of the wardrobe.

Now she had an impulse to pull it off simply because it reminded her of everything that had happened there.

Then she told herself that she had only two gowns apart from those that Katherine had given her.

She was therefore being very foolish.

It would have been equally foolish not to wear the beautiful gowns that Katherine had sent with her when she had left London.

But she could not imagine there would be anybody to appreciate them, so she left them in the trunk.

"You've got some pretty things there, dearie," Nanny said when she made the bed. "Aren't you going to hang them up?"

"Yes, of course, Nanny, as soon as I have time," Lavina had answered. "It was very kind of Katherine to think of me."

"And about time too, if you asks me!" Nanny said sharply.

She left the bed-room and did not mention the gowns again.

Lavina knew she was still resenting the way Katherine had neglected her after she had gone to London.

"She tried to make up for it by taking me to Sherwood Park," she told herself. "How I wish she had not done so."

That was untrue.

She knew that, although to think of him and long for him was agonising, she would never, never be sorry that she had met the Marquis.

She went downstairs and thought she would read a book.

Because it had been cold, she had come in earlier than she usually did.

She put some logs on the fire.

She was just about to sit down in a comfortable chair to try to concentrate on her book when she heard a rat-tat on the front-door.

She wondered if Nanny would hear it.

If not, she would have to answer it herself.

Then she heard Nanny's footsteps in the hall and wondered who the caller could be.

She expected it would be somebody from the village and hoped they had not called to see her father.

He had been doing what he called his "Parish Work" all the morning.

Now he had retired to his Study to continue work on his book.

It would upset him to be disturbed.

'Perhaps it is somebody I can see for him,' Lavina thought.

Then the door of the Sitting-Room opened and Nanny said:

"The Marquis of Sherwood to see you, Miss Lavina!"

For a moment Lavina, who had been looking into the fire, could not move.

Then, as she turned her head, she saw that it really was the Marquis.

He seemed to fill the whole room and looked taller and more broad-shouldered than she remembered.

As he walked slowly towards her she felt as if she could not breathe.

He reached her, then, as he did not speak, she said in a voice that did not sound like her own:

"Why . . . why are you . . . here? What . . . has happened? How . . . did you . . . find me?"

"So many questions," the Marquis said, "but I think I should be asking them, not you!"

He was looking at her in a penetrating manner which made her feel as if he saw into the very depths of her soul.

"How can you have done anything so absurd and outrageous as to pretend to be a Gaiety Girl?" he asked.

He spoke angrily.

Lavina felt herself tremble and was afraid of the expression in his eyes.

There was silence as he waited for her answer.

"H-how...could you have...found me?" she asked. "Surely, it was not...Rupert who...told you?"

"Rupert lies very convincingly," the Marquis replied. "But I want you to tell me how, after what we have been through together, you could go off in that sneaking, surreptitious manner without saying good-bye and without telling me the truth."

"W-we left so...early," Lavina said, "because we did not want...you to know...who we were."

"I can understand that as far as the others are concerned," the Marquis said, "but not you."

"You said 'the...others,'" Lavina murmured. "Do you...know who they...really are?"

"I found out what happened by using my intelligence," the Marquis said "and no one but you is aware of what I have discovered."

Lavina looked at him in surprise.

"Do you...mean that?"

"*I* have a habit of speaking the truth!" the Marquis said. "I have come to you for an explanation before seeing anybody else."

Lavina twisted her fingers together.

"I cannot...understand how you have...discovered...me. I was...lying to...you, but, please... it would be best for you not to...know anything...

142

but just . . . to go away and . . . forget it."

To her surprise the Marquis laughed.

"Do you really think that is possible?" he asked. "How can I spend the rest of my life not being curious and not trying to find an explanation?"

"If . . . if I tell you . . . about me," Lavina asked, "will that be . . . enough?"

"It is certainly something I want to hear," the Marquis said. "I think it is a mistake, Vina, or perhaps I should say 'Lavina,' for us to have secrets from each other."

Lavina thought there was a very big secret between them and one that he must never know.

It was that she loved him.

Because she felt as if her legs could no longer support her, she sat down on the sofa.

"It is . . . a little . . . complicated," she murmured.

The Marquis continued standing, but now with his back to the fire.

"The complications are of your making," he said, "therefore you must unravel them by telling me the truth."

"What . . . what do you want . . . to know . . . first?" Lavina asked weakly.

"I want to know how you could go away without telling me you were going, knowing I would never be able to find you again."

"But . . . you have . . . found me!"

"With the greatest difficulty."

There was a silence. Then Lavina said:

"I thought . . . perhaps you would . . . not be interested enough to want to . . . see me again . . . once I had . . . left."

"Did you really think that?" the Marquis asked. "And were you quite content for me to forget you, as you thought I would forget you?"

Lavina remembered how she had cried every night into her pillow, how lonely and miserable she had been these last days.

The Marquis was waiting for an answer, and after a moment she said:

"I . . . I knew I could not . . . do what you asked me to do . . . and therefore . . . the only thing . . . possible was not to . . . see you."

"What I suggested was entirely your fault," the Marquis said. "You were pretending to be what you are not, and in fact you bewildered me with everything you said and everything you did."

"And yet . . . you wanted to . . . see me again?" Lavina asked in a very small voice.

"Of course I wanted to see you!" the Marquis said positively. "When I learnt you had hidden yourself so completely, I knew it was going to be very difficult."

"Then . . . how did you find me?" Lavina enquired.

The Marquis smiled.

"I went back to London on Monday afternoon and called at the Gaiety Theatre. I saw George Edwardes and asked him where *The Girl* was playing next."

Lavina gave a little exclamation because she had not thought of him doing that.

"George Edwardes," the Marquis went on, "told me that it was already being performed in Manchester and handed me a programme."

Lavina gave a little cry.

"And none of our . . . names were on it!"

"So I found!" the Marquis said grimly.

"But you did not...say anything to...anyone? You did not tell...your friends?"

She spoke anxiously, knowing how much such a discovery could hurt Katherine and, of course, Millicent.

"As it happens," the Marquis answered, "when I left George Edwardes I went back to my house in Grosvenor Square because I wanted to think. I knew Rupert had lied to me and I was still wondering how I was going to find you."

Lavina drew in her breath.

So he had thought about her! He had wanted to see her again!

She felt as if the stone that had lain in her breast ever since she had come home was gradually melting.

"I went into my Study, which is similar to the one at Sherwood Park," the Marquis went on. "I was thinking of the Emerald Buddha and what it had meant to you even before the Lama arrived. Then I saw, almost as if it were being pointed out to me, a copy of *Debrett's Peerage*."

Lavina looked at him in surprise, but she did not speak and he continued:

"It suddenly struck me—or perhaps the Emerald Buddha was helping me to find you—that there was a distinct resemblance between Rupert Wick and the Girl called Kathy."

Lavina gave a little exclamation.

"I quickly looked up the Earl of Kenwick," the Marquis went on, "and found that he had a daughter called Katherine, aged eighteen. I stared at it thinking that what I was imagining might have happened was impossible. How could any *débutante* of eighteen presented at Court pretend to be a Gaiety Girl and ride as well as Kathy had when she took the jumps on my race-course?"

He made it sound so incredulous that Lavina could not help smiling even though she was nervous.

"It struck me," the Marquis was continuing, "or else again the Buddha was guiding me—that 'Vern' was an unusual name, although the name Vernon was known to me. I turned a few pages of *Debrett* and discovered that the Honourable Anthony Vernon, brother of the present Earl, was Vicar of Little Wichingford and had a daughter called Lavina!"

Lavina made an expressive gesture with her hands.

"So it was as easy as that!"

"I knew where Rupert lived and I also remembered that you had seemed very attached to Kathy. You always came downstairs together and you continually looked at her as if for reassurance."

"You ... you were aware of ... that?"

"I was aware of a great many things about you," the Marquis said, "most of all, that you were, without exception, the most beautiful person I have ever seen!"

Lavina drew in her breath. Then she said:

"You found me ... and it was very ... very clever of you ... but you do understand that it would ... hurt Katherine and all the other girls if it was ... ever known what ... they had done."

"Why did they do it?" the Marquis asked.

Lavina's eyes flickered, and she looked away from him.

"I do not ... want to ... tell you ... that."

"Why not?" he enquired.

"Because," she said, "it is very ... embarrassing for ... me."

"I do not understand, and quite frankly, I intend to know the truth, so if you prefer I will ask Kathy— or, rather, Lady Katherine."

"No, no ... of course I ... will tell ... you," Lavina said, "but you must ... promise not to be ... angry."

"I think I have every right to be angry," the Marquis said. "You come to my house and all eight of you deceive me and my friends intending, of course, to make fools of us."

"O-only of ... you," Lavina murmured.

"Only of me? But why me? What have I done to hurt you?"

Lavina took a deep breath.

Then she said in a voice the Marquis could hardly hear:

"When Rupert told you that Katherine had ... invited you to a party ... you said ... if there was one thing you ... avoided it was ... half-witted ... gauche ... stupid and not very educated *débutantes* ..."

Her voice died away on the last word.

She dared not look at the Marquis because she thought he would be so angry.

Unexpectedly he threw back his head and laughed.

"I do not believe it!" he said. "Do you mean to say this whole masquerade was simply because I said that?"

"Katherine was furious and she decided to show

you that *débutantes* could be intelligent and because you would not meet them the only thing was to be disguised as the women you really enjoyed being with."

"I see her reasoning," the Marquis said, "and now I understand a great many things that were puzzling me before."

"Then...you are...not angry?" Lavina asked.

"Only with you," he replied.

"Then...please," Lavina said, "you do...promise not to betray...any of the other girls...or let any of your...friends know that they were...not who they...pretended to...be?"

"You mean it would damage their reputation?"

"Of course it would!" Lavina said. "And we were...staying there without a...chaperone."

"Which was indeed extremely reprehensible!" the Marquis reflected.

She thought there was something grim about the way he spoke.

Perhaps he would tell people what had happened, just to teach them all a lesson.

"None of our...parents had the...slightest idea of what we were...doing," she said, "and they would be very...very...angry."

"Of course they would!" the Marquis agreed.

"Millicent has become engaged to the Earl of Morne," Lavina continued, "and it was he who... insisted that Rupert should not tell...you the truth, which Katherine had...arranged for him to do... after we left."

"So I *was* to know the truth!" the Marquis remarked.

"Only to teach . . . you a lesson . . . then Rupert was sure you would . . . behave like a gentleman and not . . . tell anybody else."

"The whole idea was crazy from the very beginning!" The Marquis said. "At the same time, I have to commend you on looking not only like Gaiety Girls, but very much more beautiful and attractive than they could possibly be!"

"Did you . . . really think . . . that?"

"I certainly thought it where you were concerned," the Marquis answered.

Lavina blushed. Then she said:

"As I am not . . . important, it does not . . . matter that . . . you have . . . found me out . . . but please . . . please . . . keep all the other . . . girls a secret!"

"I am not really concerned with them," the Marquis replied, "but with you."

Lavina gave a little cry.

"You would not tell Papa? He would be very . . . shocked and also . . . hurt that I should do . . . anything so . . . deceitful."

"Then why did you agree?" the Marquis enquired.

Lavina looked at him in surprise.

"Surely you can . . . understand. It has been . . . lonely . . . here while Katherine has been in . . . London. I had not seen her for nearly . . . a year and when she came back and asked me to . . . help her by being the eighth 'Gaiety Girl' and come and stay with you . . . it was the most . . . exciting thing that has . . . ever happened!"

"And you have never been to London?" the Marquis asked.

"Only when I stayed two or three nights with

Katherine while we had the special gowns made which were to disguise us as the sort of women you prefer to be with."

"So you told me the truth when you said you had never been kissed!" the Marquis said quietly.

Lavina remembered what else he had asked her, and she blushed.

"I never thought...I never imagined," she said, "when I...locked my door that anyone would... come to my...bed-room!"

The Marquis did not answer, and after a moment she exclaimed:

"That other door...is that the...reason my room was...changed?"

"I thought you would guess that sooner or later," the Marquis answered.

Lavina's cheeks were crimson as he added:

"You cannot blame me if you are such a very good actress!"

"I...I am only just...beginning to...understand why Katherine said we must all...lock our doors. She must have...known that...sort of thing... happened to...Gaiety Girls!"

"Forget it," the Marquis said. "You were punished for being deceitful. Until I came to you that night I thought your air of innocence and ignorance was all part of the act."

"I do see it was...very wrong...of me," Lavina murmured.

"But then," the Marquis went on, "you were brave enough to come to my room and tell me I was wanted by the Emerald Buddha. How could you have known that?"

"I think you ... know the ... answer," Lavina murmured. "I told you when I first ... held it that I ... felt as if it was ... speaking to me. Even now I can hardly ... believe I have touched ... anything so ... wonderful ... and I shall never forget the ... blessing the Lama ... gave us."

"Neither will I," the Marquis said unexpectedly. "But I want to know, Lavina, how you thought you could forget me."

"I ... I did not say I could ... forget you," Lavina answered, "but I ... thought I would never ... see you again."

"And that did not worry you?"

She drew in her breath and looked down.

Then, as she realised he wanted an answer, she said:

"Of course I ... wanted ... to see you! But I thought it would be ... impossible because ... then you would ... know that we had ... acted out Katherine's Charade."

"A very reprehensible one," the Marquis said.

"I ... I am sorry ... will you ever ... forgive me and please ... do not be ... angry with me ... anymore."

She spoke to him pleadingly.

As she looked up at him, her eyes beseeching him, he put out his hands and pulled her to her feet.

Before she realised what was happening, his arms were round her.

Then his lips came down on hers.

Because she had been so unhappy and so worried, she could hardly believe what was happening.

Now the stars were back in her breast and the

ecstasy she had felt when she held the Emerald Buddha was also there.

The Marquis kissed her at first gently.

Then as he felt the softness and sweetness of her lips and that her body seemed to melt into his, his kiss became more demanding, more possessive.

To Lavina it was as if the clouds parted and he carried her into a special Heaven.

As he kissed her and went on kissing her, the Marquis knew that never in his whole life had he felt such strange and yet wonderful sensations as her lips gave him.

Only when Lavina felt it impossible to feel such rapture and yet still be alive did the Marquis raise his head.

"I love you, my darling!" he said. "How soon will you marry me?"

As he spoke he saw once again the radiance on Lavina's face which had held him spellbound when she was worshipping the Emerald Buddha.

Then the expression on her face faded.

In a broken little voice he could hardly hear she said:

"I ... I love you ... but ... I cannot ... marry you!"

The Marquis never thought it possible that any woman he wanted to marry would refuse him, and especially not Lavina.

"Why will you not marry me?" he asked. "You love me, I know you love me!"

"I love you with ... all my heart and ... soul," Lavina whispered, "but if we were ... married, you would ... soon become ... bored with me ... and then I ... would want ... only to ... die."

The Marquis pulled her closer to him.

"Why do you say that when I have told you that I love you?" he asked. "I swear I have never loved anyone as I love you."

"But...I am not a Gaiety Girl," Lavina said with a little sob. "I only...pretended to be...one."

Gently the Marquis led her to the sofa and said as she sat down:

"I have to make you understand and therefore I am going to tell you something I have never talked about before."

Again he was standing with his back to the fire and he went on:

"I know exactly what you are thinking about my behaviour with the Gaiety Girls, and I am quite aware that people laugh at what they call my 'obsession' with them."

"You...know that?"

"Of course I know it," he said. "I am not a fool!"

"N-no...of course not...but...I do not...understand."

The Marquis gave a little sigh, then, as if he felt what he wanted to say had to be said, he began:

"My mother died when I was ten. I adored her, she was everything that was soft, gentle, and loving in my life. After her death my father, because I was an only child, took over my training."

His lips tightened before he went on:

"'Training' is the right word! My father was determined I should be trained for the position I would hold when he died so that I would be the cleverest and most distinguished Marquis of Sherwood there has ever been!"

He spoke in a hard voice.

Because Lavina knew it was hurting him to tell her this, she said:

"If telling ... me this upsets you ... I would ra-ther ... you did not ... say any ... more."

"You have to know the truth," the Marquis said quietly.

There was a pause before he continued:

"My father insisted that even at the holidays I have Tutors who worked me so hard that I had little time to play, but because I was stuffed with knowl-edge I became Head Boy at Eton."

He sighed and went on:

"When I went to Oxford I was awarded a First Class Degree, having again spent my holidays study-ing with Tutors."

"When I went into the Household Brigade my fa-ther was determined I should become a General."

His voice was harsh as he said:

"He chose my books. Every available minute I was not in Barracks I spent learning the History of the Army down the centuries. When I was not in Bar-racks I met the men who talked of nothing else but Regimental customs and the battles in which the Regiment had fought."

There was a bitterness in the Marquis's face which told Lavina how irksome it had all been.

"My father drove and drove me," he said, "until unexpectedly he died. That happened four years ago and after the Funeral I realised that I was free: Free of being pushed, pressured, and forced to strive every minute of my life for some prized position I did not want myself, but which pleased him."

The Marquis walked across to the window and back again as if he were thinking.

Then he said:

"Perhaps you can understand that once I realised I was free I became like a little boy let loose in a Sweet-shop. For the first time in my life I was my own master. Of course I wanted to laugh at things that were nonsensical and had no serious message behind them."

He paused for breath before he went on:

"But most of all, I intended to avoid being married."

Lavina's eyes widened and he said:

"Just before he died my father had been busy choosing me a wife, determined that I should marry somebody who would be an advantage to the family and who would glorify my position, if it was possible, in the Social World."

The Marquis said ironically:

"Fortunately he died before he could make the ultimate choice, but he had two or three candidates in mind!"

Lavina was beginning to realise where this story was leading.

"Being mindful of my social position," the Marquis continued, "I knew that every ambitious mama would thrust her daughters on me, and if I was not careful I would be caught in the trap which my father had already prepared for me."

"So you went ... instead to ... the Gaiety," Lavina said in a whisper.

"Exactly!" the Marquis agreed. "I went to the

Gaiety and found the fun and pleasure I had been denied for so long."

He laughed ruefully.

"I found amusement with the Gaiety Girls who were safe to be with because they could not entrap me so that I could never escape."

"I...I understand," Lavina said, "of course I... understand."

"As soon as one bored me I went on to another," the Marquis said as if he must convince her further. "I paid generously for my pleasure, and it was like changing my toys, or choosing another horse. There were a few tears, but no recriminations."

There was silence before he said in a different tone of voice:

"It all seemed everything I wanted—until I met you."

Lavina felt herself quiver as his voice deepened.

"I think I fell in love with you," he said, "that first night at dinner when you admired my Dining-Room and I wanted you to admire me."

"But, of course I did!" Lavina said. "At the same time, I was...frightened of...you."

"I can understand that."

"But...you were different from what I expected."

"In what way?"

"You were kind, and nobody had said that about you...and it was not...only what you said, but what I...felt when I was...near you."

"What did you feel?"

"It is difficult to...explain, but when you first... shook my hand I was aware of...strange vibrations...rather the same as...what I felt when I was... touching the... Emerald Buddha."

"You perplexed, bemused, and bewildered me," the Marquis said, "and when you rode so well you looked so exceedingly beautiful I knew I had to protect you."

Lavina blushed.

Then she said very quietly:

"But you must... realise that if... we were married... and you wished to... choose... somebody else... you will not be able to... pay me to... go away."

The Marquis smiled.

"Do you really think, my darling, I would want anybody other than you?"

"But... you might... then I should feel that I had... trapped you... and however hard I tried... I would be unable to... set you free."

Lavina's voice broke on the last words, and tears were in her eyes.

The Marquis moved forward and pulled her into his arms.

"How could I ever be bored with you or want to change you for somebody else?" he asked. "You are mine, Lavina, mine completely and absolutely! We were not only joined from the first moment we met, but immutably by the blessing of the Lama."

Lavina looked up at him.

"That was... what I thought, but I did not think you... would feel it... too."

"Of course I feel it," the Marquis said. "I have never known anything so strange and at the same time so wonderful."

He looked at her tenderly as he went on:

"I knew he had made us one person and it would

be impossible for us ever to lose each other."

Lavina put her head against his shoulder.

Then he exclaimed:

"You are crying, my darling! Why does that make you unhappy?"

"I am crying because I am...so happy!" Lavina sobbed. "I thought I had...lost you and you would...forget me...and I would...never be able to...l-love anybody else...ever again!"

"And you never will," the Marquis said. "You will love me and be with me, and be mine for the rest of our lives!"

Then he was kissing her, kissing her wildly, passionately, demandingly, and the stars in her heart became little flames.

$$* \quad * \quad *$$

It was a long time later that the Marquis said:

"I think, my precious, I must talk to your father and ask him to marry us at once."

"A-at...once?" Lavina stammered.

He pulled her a little closer before he said:

"You are being very silly! You know as well as I do that if we announce our engagement and arrange a big wedding, every man who was staying with me for the shooting-party will recognise you."

"I had...forgotten...that," Lavina said. "Oh, darling, how can I...marry you?"

"Very easily," the Marquis replied. "We will be married to-morrow morning by your father. Then we are going away immediately on a very long honeymoon."

He paused before he said:

"I cannot take you to Tibet, but I think you will enjoy India and, of course, as I missed going to Sār-nāth, where the Buddha preached his first Sermon, you will have to take me there."

Lavina gave a cry of sheer joy.

"Do you mean that . . . do you really . . . mean it?"

"Of course I mean it!" the Marquis said. "And I can imagine nothing more exciting, my darling, than taking you to India and a great many other places that until now you have seen only in your imagination."

"This is not true . . . it cannot be true . . . I am dreaming!" Lavina said in a broken little voice.

"From now on we will dream together, and we will be the two happiest people in the world," the Marquis said.

He kissed away the tears on her cheeks.

Then he said:

"What are we waiting for? If your father is in his Study writing his book, we must go and tell him what we have planned."

"But . . . not about staying in . . . your house?"

"Of course not," the Marquis said. "I met you in London at a very respectable dinner-party given by Katherine and Rupert Wick, and I fell in love with you at first sight—that is true, at any rate!"

"I will . . . never lie . . . again," Lavina vowed.

"I will make sure of that," the Marquis said, "but if you had not been trying to prove that a *débutante* is cleverer than a Gaiety Girl, we might never have met."

Lavina laughed.

"Rupert said all that Katherine had proved was

that *débutantes* had brains."

"But you, my precious, have both beauty and brains," the Marquis said, "so I have nothing to complain about!"

"I hope that is what you will . . . always say about me," Lavina said.

"I will say a lot more things besides," the Marquis said, "but you will have to wait until we are married. Oh, my darling, I adore you so much that it is going to be hard to wait until to-morrow!"

Lavina laughed as she rose to her feet.

"We will go and tell Papa at once, and we must promise to bring him back more information about India to add to his book."

He had no sooner said the last word before the Marquis had his arms around her and was kissing her.

"I adore you! I love you! I worship you!" he said. "We have been blessed, more than any other people in the world because we have found each other."

"That is true," Lavina whispered, "and I love you because you are so wonderful . . . so kind . . . so generous . . . so everything a man should be."

The last words were lost against the Marquis's lips.

He kissed her until the room was whirling round her.

They seemed to be floating high in the sky among the stars, and the Light that the Lama had given them enveloped them both.

It was the Light that comes from Eternity and is Eternal.

The Light of Love.

ABOUT THE AUTHOR

Barbara Cartland, the world's most famous romantic novelist, who is also an historian, playwright, lecturer, political speaker and television personality, has now written over 530 books and sold nearly 500 million copies all over the world.

She has also had many historical works published and has written four autobiographies as well as the biographies of her mother and that of her brother, Ronald Cartland, who was the first Member of Parliament to be killed in the last war. This book has a preface by Sir Winston Churchill and has just been republished with an introduction by Sir Arthur Bryant.

Love at the Helm, a novel written with the help and inspiration of the late Earl Mountbatten of Burma, Great Uncle of His Royal Highness The Prince of Wales, is being sold for the Mountbatten Memorial Trust.

She has broken the world record for the last fourteen years by writing an average of twenty-three books a year. In the *Guinness Book of Records* she is listed as the world's top-selling author.

Miss Cartland in 1978 sang an Album of Love Songs with the Royal Philharmonic Orchestra.

In private life Barbara Cartland, who is a Dame of the Order of St. John of Jerusalem, Chairman of the

St. John Council in Hertfordshire and Deputy President of the St. John Ambulance Brigade, has fought for better conditions and salaries for Midwives and Nurses.

She championed the cause for the Elderly in 1956 invoking a Government Enquiry into the "Housing Conditions of Old People."

In 1962 she had the Law of England changed so that Local Authorities had to provide camps for their own Gypsies. This has meant that since then thousands and thousands of Gypsy children have been able to go to School, which they had never been able to do in the past, as their caravans were moved every twenty-four hours by the Police.

There are now fourteen camps in Hertfordshire and Barbara Cartland has her own Romany Gypsy Camp called Barbaraville by the Gypsies.

Her designs "Decorating with Love" were sold all over the U.S.A. and the National Home Fashions League made her, in 1981, "Women of Achievement."

She is unique in that she was one and two in the Dalton list of Best Sellers, and one week had four books in the top twenty.

Barbara Cartland's book *Getting Older, Growing Younger* has been published in Great Britain and the U.S.A. and her fifth cookery book, *The Romance of Food*, is now being used by the House of Commons.

In 1984 she received at Kennedy Airport America's Bishop Wright Air Industry Award for her contribution to the development of aviation. In 1931 she and two R.A.F. Officers thought of, and carried, the first aeroplane-towed glider airmail.

During the War she was Chief Lady Welfare Officer in Bedfordshire looking after 20,000 Service men and women. She thought of having a pool of Wedding Dresses at the War Office so a Service Bride could hire a gown for the day.

She bought 1,000 gowns without coupons for the A.T.S., the W.A.A.F.'s and the W.R.E.N.S. In 1945 Barbara Cartland received the Certificate of Merit from Eastern Command.

In 1964 Barbara Cartland founded the National Association for Health of which she is the President, as a front for all the Health Stores and for any product made as alternative medicine.

This is now a £650,000 turnover a year, with one third going in export.

In January 1988 she received *La Médaille de Vermeil de la Ville de Paris*. This is the highest award to be given in France by the City of Paris. She has sold 25 million books in France.

In March 1988 Barbara Cartland was asked by the Indian Government to open their health resort outside Delhi. This is almost the largest health resort in the world.

Barbara Cartland was received with great enthusiasm by her fans, who fêted her at a reception in the City and she received the gift of an embossed plate from the Government.